# davida wills hurwin

Inspired by real events in the lives of
**Matthew Boger and Tim Zaal**

LITTLE, BROWN AND COMPANY

New York   Boston

Copyright © 2009 by Davida Wills Hurwin

Little, Brown and Company

Hachette Book Group
1290 Avenue of the Americas, New York, NY 10104
Visit our website at www.lb-teens.com

Little, Brown and Company is a division of Hachette Book Group, Inc.
The Little, Brown name and logo are trademarks of Hachette Book Group, Inc.

The publisher is not responsible for websites (or their content) that are not owned by the publisher.

First Paperback Edition: June 2012
First published in hardcover in November 2009 by Little, Brown and Company

Library of Congress Cataloging-In-Publication Data

Hurwin, Davida, 1950–
Freaks and Revelations : a novel / by Davida Wills Hurwin.—1st ed.
   p. cm.
"Inspired by real events in the lives of Matthew Boger and Tim Zaal."
Summary: Tells, in two voices, of events leading up to a 1980 incident in which fourteen-year-old Jason, a gay youth surviving on the streets as a prostitute, and seventeen-year-old Doug, a hate-filled punk rocker, have a fateful meeting in a Los Angeles alley.
ISBN 978-0-316-04996-2 (hc) / ISBN 978-0-316-04997-9 (pb)
[1. Hate—Fiction. 2. Prejudices—Fiction. 3. Homosexuality—Fiction. 4. Punk culture—Fiction. 5. Family problems—Fiction. 6. Drug abuse—Fiction. 7. California—History—20th century—Fiction.] I. Title.
PZ7.H95735Fre 2009
[Fic]—dc22
                                                                          2008047384

10 9 8 7 6 5 4 3 2

LSC-H

Printed in the United States of America

For my daughter,
Frazier Malone

In loving memory of my second mom,
Frances Grace Williams

I know where I am by the sounds

that play rhythms like raindrops through tin pipes,

moonlight that falls in secret messages, and

echoes of invitations to places unknown.

I am strong here; I am the all of me,

the beginning and the celebration,

the promise and the reward;

I am not afraid, not now.

Not anymore.

I am a child and I believe.

I am a child and all things are possible.


Thoughts of a boy before sunrise

On March 27, 1980, a horrible thing happened.

I never saw a kid that night;
I saw a creature, an enemy, taking something that belonged
to me. That's not an excuse, I know—there is no excuse,
no good reason. It's not an apology either. Apologies
don't really help. The thing is done. I did it.

# 1973

SEVEN YEARS BEFORE

LOS ANGELES COUNTY, CALIFORNIA

{1}

"Stupid kid. Stupid, stupid, *stupid* kid."

My dad: muttering, pacing, dark, starting to swell, making my heart beat even faster than it already does from running. Mom's nowhere in sight, even though it was her that called us. Henry's dad watches from the lawn. He reminds me of a rabbit caught in headlights.

"Are we in trouble?" Henry whispers to the back of my ear. We stand at the edge of his driveway, trying to catch our breath, both of us clutching our action figures.

"Shhhh." I poke him with my David Steele.

"I told you we'd get caught."

"So what."

He tries to take my hand but I cross my arms in front of my chest. This isn't like when we were little, before he moved, when we did Indian Guides together. We're *ten* now, I'll be eleven in a couple of months. Boys don't hold hands.

My dad snaps his head toward us. I hold my breath, back up into Henry. Why didn't I listen? Why did I make Henry go down to those old wells anyway? Was it that great to have David Steele and Big Jim be able to smash up all that dirt?

Yeah, it was. The dirt sods were the best I ever saw. Just right for action figures, just like Henry said. I pushed the button on David Steele's back and *THWACK*—his arm swung over and slammed his iron pipe into the dirt, *HARD*. Henry's guy did the same with his axe. But we snuck down, nobody saw us go. How did they know we were there?

Without warning, my dad turns and stomps toward the car.

"What's wrong with him?" my friend whispers.

I glance over. Can Henry see him swelling up?

"He gets like this sometimes."

Now he's in the car, backing it toward us, fast, the rear tires sliding back and forth on the dirt. Henry's dad grabs our shoulders, edges us up onto the grass. Our moms come out on the porch. Mine holds my pirate suitcase and her big red leather one. What's going on?

"I thought you were staying till Sunday," Henry says. I shrug.

His mom whispers something to mine, who shakes her head no, and then smiles that stupid frozen smile she gets when she's scared or doesn't know what to do. My stomach cramps up. Something bad has happened. Something way worse than us two guys playing down by the wells.

"Both of you," my father barks, pointing first at Mom, then at me, "in the car."

I take two steps and remember my sleeping bag spread out on the floor in Henry's room, the brand new *expensive* sleeping bag I begged for and almost didn't get because my dad said I'd mess it up. I dash to the house, slide down the wood floor in the hallway to Henry's room, and snatch up the bag. I'll be in that car before my mom even crosses the yard. With a grin on my face, I fly out the door, right into my huge glaring pissed-off father.

"WHAT. DID. I. SAY." The words come from the back of his throat, low and scary, like a pit bull growling. Henry hears and his eyes bug out.

My dad vice-grips my arm and drags me stumbling backwards across the yard. I drop the bag and almost lose David Steele. He tosses me into the backseat of the car and slams the door. Of course I land on my bad hip, but I manage not to cry out. Henry's mom scurries to pick up the bag and Mom opens the front car door to receive it. Too late—we're moving, leaving Henry and his parents in a haze of dust. Mom just manages to close her door before we turn onto the street. I look back through the rear window. I wave to Henry, but he doesn't wave back.

Tucking David Steele under my arm, I fasten my seat belt, not easy to do with my dad lurching around corners. My hip hurts from landing on it. Nobody's telling me anything. Dad runs a red light, then another, making the tires squeal as we zoom onto the ramp and over to the freeway.

"Please slow down, Roger," my mom begs. She's got that same frozen smile. I hate that smile. I hate how her voice changes, how her back slumps. If I said something now, she wouldn't hear it—she's only hearing *him*.

"You want out?" Dad growls.

"No, I just—"

"Maybe you wanna walk home?"

"No. But, Roger—" Her voice creeps even higher.

"Shut up then, okay? Can you shut up for once?" He cuts across three lanes of traffic and the back of a big blue car materializes in front of us, maybe two feet away. Mom makes a funny little sound and Dad brakes, throwing us both forwards. Mom bashes her head on the window frame. I grunt as I smack my face into the back of her seat. Dad guns it and I slam back, hard. I peek at the speedometer: eighty-five. My mom doesn't talk again.

\*       \*       \*

"He's stupid," my dad blurts, loudly, suddenly, startling me. "Just plain *stupid*." It seems we've been driving for hours. My gut and my heart both clench up. Does he mean me?

"He didn't know," Mom says.

"The kid's seventeen years old, Mary. I told him to stay away from there. He knew. Okay?" He snorts, shakes his head. "Serves him right, getting shot. Maybe now he'll listen."

Something happens to the air around me; it shimmers like the air off sidewalks on hot days, and suddenly there isn't enough of it to breathe.

My brother is shot?

I hear the words. I can't seem to put together what they mean.

"He'll be all right," Mom says.

"Yeah? Who died and made you God?"

Mom starts crying, whimpering really, her shoulders bouncing up and down, her hand covering her face. Every little while, she blows her nose.

My brother is shot.

Is he dead?

Can Carl be dead?

I imagine bullets flying, hitting Carl, then whizzing through the air, looking for the rest of us. If Carl can be shot, so can we. If Carl can die, anyone can. Even us. My dad weaves and cusses. Mom cries. My hands shake, then my arms. Then my whole body. I taste vomit in the back of my throat and I swallow it back down. Better that than face my dad if I puke in his car. He's swelled so big now I don't know how he fits in the seat.

I hold David Steele as tight as I can and pray for him to turn life-size. I want him to be huge, bigger even than my dad. He can slide over and sit next to me, right behind my dad's seat. Except my dad won't be able to see him. Just me. We'll wait. When the time's right, David Steele will turn his head and we'll smile at each other. Both of us will know exactly what's coming next. We'll wait a bit more, until Dad pulls off the freeway and maybe stops at the stoplight or even until he turns into our driveway.

David Steele will look over again and this time he'll wink.

I'll nod and wink back.

I won't even need to push the button.

## {2}

"Don't let him be dead, don't let him be dead," Grams mutters over and over, pacing the living room. It took three and a half hours for us to get back from Henry's ranch. My head feels weird, like there's a motor running inside it. Everybody else is at the hospital: Mom, Dad, Grandpa, my sister, Chelsea, and of course, Carl. I'm not allowed because I'm too young. Grams has to stay with me. The TV's on, but I'm not watching, just staring in that general direction. I'm listening to my grandma. I want to know what's going on.

The phone rings. Grams stops moving and her face goes pale. I hold David Steele close to my chest, like he could make my heart stop pounding. With a glance at me, Grams ignores the phone on the table and lumbers into the kitchen to take the call. I know it's my mom. I gulp in air and blow it out.

"Hello?" Grams says. Her voice sounds crackly. I'd get up and turn the TV down, but then she'd know I'm listening.

*"Here's the story of a man named Brady . . ."*

I turn my ear toward the kitchen. It doesn't help: she's whispering.

"Please don't let him be dead," I echo.

*     *     *

It feels like forever until Grams comes back in. Her face is worse, gray and tight. Looking at her makes my stomach clench. When I breathe, inside me is an earthquake.

"A nigger shot him," she mumbles.

She's not talking to me, I know that. She doesn't look at me; it's like I'm not there. She wipes her mouth hard, sighs, plops down on the couch with a groan, and reaches for the wine bottle. It's empty. "Damn it," she growls and now looks in my direction. "Get my bottle from the fridge," she orders. I jump up and dash for the kitchen. I bring both the wine and the opener.

She's holding David Steele. I set the bottle down and reach for him. She smirks as she hands him off, with the exact same face my grandpa gets when he's talking to Dad. She stabs the corkscrew into the top of the cork, twists like she wants to hurt someone. "You're ten years old, Douglas. Does your father know you play with dolls?"

"He's not a doll. He's an *action figure*. I don't play with dolls." I whisper it, but it wouldn't matter if I yelled. She isn't listening.

"What's this world coming to?" She pulls out the cork. "I don't know anymore. I just don't know." Grams fills her glass to the top. "Decent people getting shot." She downs it.

I slip off the couch with David Steele and scoot on my butt around the corner, leaning against the side. I hate Grams when she drinks. I hate having to be alone with her—she always makes fun of me. I hate that she said that word. It makes me think we're still not safe. It's a bad word. When my father says it, Mom makes him shush.

I push David Steele's button—*thwack!!*

Is Carl dead? No, then she'd be crying.

I push again. *Thwack!!!*

But he's shot. My brother is shot. A bad guy shot him, right over by my old school. Exactly where I used to cross the street with Larry, the crossing guard. I don't want to think about it but I don't know how to stop. My brain plays it over and over: *A bad guy shot my brother, a bad guy shot my brother.* I look behind me; I'm not sure why except now I know bad guys are everywhere. They find you even when you move.

*THWACK.*

We're supposed to be safe in this house. There aren't supposed to be cholas here, like in Pomona. No black people, either. A few Orientals, but they don't bother anybody. Good thing my father could see the handwriting on the wall, that's what Mom said. Things were changing where we used to live. White people had to look out for themselves. Cholas were everywhere.

Cholas are like Mexicans, but worse. They hate white people. I never saw one, but I heard my sister talk about them, and I figured out that they're probably a lot like Medusa from *Sinbad and the Seven Seas*, which I used to watch all the time when I was little. Except, instead of snakes for hair, they've got sharp shiny razorblades hanging onto long black strands.

When we lived in Pomona, they took over Chelsea's high school. Me and Mom found this out when Chels came home crying. She never cried, so I knew right off that it was bad. Really bad. I listened to her tell Mom how she almost got beat up. How her friend did get smacked, right in the head. How Chels never wanted to go back. I could just see it: cholas standing up on top of the lockers in the girls' gym room, like Medusa on the cliffs, waiting for the white girls to come by.

*THWACK! THWACK!!!*

I peek around the couch. Grams is sitting up, head lolling to the side, snoring. Her glass is tipped; drops of wine look like blood on the couch. What will happen now? Will we move again? Will Carl be okay? Will more black guys try to shoot more white people? Will the cholas come and take over our schools here too?

What if they come to our house?

Pomona isn't far. Carl goes back there all the time to hang out with friends. At least he used to. He might not anymore, not after being shot. But what if he wasn't careful what he said to people? Maybe the bad guys found out where we live. My dad has a gun. Will he shoot them? I look around. Where will I hide? I check the windows. What will I do?

I start to shiver on the outside too, even though it's not at all cold. I want to cry or have my mom here to tell me a story or sing one of the songs she used to make up when I was a little kid. But Mom's taking care of Carl. Who could die, all because of a . . .

". . . *nigger.*"

I try it out in the lowest of all whispers, then hold my breath, in case God or someone strikes me down.

"Nigger."

My lips don't even have to move, only my tongue pushing off behind my teeth. I like how the word feels in my mouth, how the sound is clear, hard. It's like pushing the button on David Steele's back.

It makes me feel strong.

It makes me feel like I know what to do.

# 1975

FIVE YEARS BEFORE

LOS ANGELES COUNTY

Mom and Carl are both in the kitchen when I get home from school. Mom's grinning. Carl isn't.

"They caught him, Dougie," Mom says. "They got the bastard that shot our Carl. Finally." She hands me the *Tribune*. "Look. It's all right there."

Carl doesn't seem all that happy about his name being in the newspaper, but Mom sure is. She rubs his shoulders and musses his hair, gives him a kiss on the back of his neck. He rolls his eyes and tries to shrug her away. She doesn't notice. He got his name in the newspaper. They caught the bad guy. This is what counts. She picks up the phone to call Chelsea. Carl ambles off to his room. I go to mine.

The only good thing about my sister moving out is that both us boys now have our own room. Carl put a black light up in his, with posters of Jimi Hendrix and Janis Joplin that change when it's on. He locks himself in there whenever he's home, to play guitar or hang out with his friends. They smoke pot when Mom and Dad are out of the house, and won't ever let me in. He ignores me when his friends are around. I'm just his stupid little brother. He makes fun of how tall and skinny I got. I don't care. Let him do what he wants, I can take care of myself. I have friends. Well, two. Besides, in seventh grade, you can get your own pot.

I miss Chels, but she likes living with her boyfriend better, anyway.

Turns out everybody at school saw the article. My homeroom teacher mentions it to me after class, asks if Carl's okay. Kids are looking at me weird, though, so I try to get ready to stick up for him, if I have to. At snack, I wait to know which way it's gonna go, when Evelyn Anderson and her friends crowd around.

Evelyn has tits already. Big ones.

"Did he really get shot?" she asks.

"Uh-huh. Right by the heart."

"Oh! Is he okay?"

"Yeah. He's fine now. But he still has the *bullet* in him."

I like how the word makes a little explosion in my mouth as it comes out, how the sound of it makes people stand very still. "Too close to his spine to operate."

I like the general "ooooh" that ripples through the group.

"Oh my God," Evelyn Anderson says.

"Yep," I answer. I'm having a hard time keeping my eyes on her face. "Now he has to go testify. In court."

"Is he scared?" her friend asks.

"Nah, not my brother."

"What if the guy gets off and comes after him again?" Evelyn asks.

"The guy who shot him? No way. He'll be doing some hard time." I heard my mom say this to my grandma, on the phone. She didn't know I was listening. "It's not his first arrest, you know. That nigger's got a record as long as your arm."

No one speaks. The air sizzles briefly and seems to take form around us; it feels heavier than a second ago. Evelyn's eyes get real big; she looks back over her shoulder. I feel my cheeks get warm.

"What?" I challenge.

"Nothing," she says, but she doesn't look in my eyes now.

"You shouldn't say that word," whispers her friend.

"What word? *Nigger?* Why not?"

"Because." Evelyn looks around. Who does she expect to see? Only white people go to this school. She whispers too. "You just shouldn't. It's not a nice word."

"He's not a nice guy."

"Still—"

"So what *should* I call him?"

"I don't know, but not that."

"Yeah, well, just wait till somebody shoots your brother. See how you feel then."

I don't know what else to do, so I walk away, my face red, feeling stupid, like I should've just kept my mouth shut. In math class, a couple of guys look at me funny, like they know something. Nobody else asks about Carl. At lunch, when I come around the corner to the picnic area with my buddy Glenn, a whole bunch of girls start giggling. Evelyn Anderson is one of them.

"Just ignore them," Glenn tells me.

Easy for him to say. He's not the one being laughed at.

After school, we go to Glenn's but his grandma comes home early and makes me leave. Fine. Nobody wants me around, what do I care. I don't feel like going home—Carl's probably there—so I head over to Caroline's house.

Caroline Tuttle was the first person I met when we moved here.

She's one of my best friends even though she goes to Catholic school and lives down almost by Pomona. I'm not supposed to hang around with her because her mom's never home, just her big brother, Evan, who dropped out of school. We lounge around on their front lawn while he works on his motorcycle. Carl'd be jealous.

"Want to go inside?" Caroline asks. Usually, this means we can make out on the bed in her mom's room.

"Nah."

"How come?"

I tell her. She gets it.

"I would have said exactly the same thing," she says. "What do those stupid girls know, anyway? Huh?"

"Yeah. Their brother didn't get shot."

"That's right. They're just bitches." She leans over and kisses me right in front of Evan. He whistles.

"Shut up!" she says to him, but she's smiling. She kisses me again. "Hey, you want me to make you a tattoo?"

"What?"

"You know—a tattoo. You said you wanted one."

That's true, I had been talking about it for a while now. "Shit yeah. I do."

"Hey, Evan?" she says.

"Gotcha covered, Babygirl."

Evan's got even more tattoos than Carl. He designs his own. He does all his friends. He got all the stuff, including the India ink. We go into the house. He boils a needle to sterilize it, and shows us how to strap it to a pencil with thread. You wind the thread around both the pencil and the needle, up to the tip almost, real tight.

"It can't wobble, or you mess up," he says, then smiles and holds it up. "Your rig." He sticks the point in a lighter flame, then wipes it with rubbing alcohol. "No fun if it gets infected."

Evan hands me a Coors and tells me to chug it. I tried my first beer way back in fifth grade, so this is no big deal, but I usually don't drink this fast. I don't really like the taste. I get dizzy immediately. He hands me another. This one goes down real smooth.

"You got a design?" he asks.

"Yep." I burp. "Sorry. I want a '13' right here." I point to the top of my forearm.

"Oh, perfect, Doug," says Caroline, "exactly where your dad can see it. And your teachers." I was actually thinking of Evelyn Anderson, but I get her point.

Evan explains it'll hurt less where it's fleshy, though after that second beer, I doubt I could even feel pain. I decide across my stomach'd be good. I lie down on an air mattress in the garage and Caroline draws a 13 in pen, right near my belly button. It looks fine and I nod. She takes her rig and dips the needle and the top of the thread wrap into the bottle of India ink. She pokes a hole. Then another. Evan watches, coaching her. She has to get under the top layer of skin but not go too deep or the ink could poison me. She dips and pokes again.

I'm wrong about the beer. The needle hurts like hell, but with Evan standing there, grinning down at me, I just suck it up. Every few punctures, Caroline wipes off the blood. Tattoos bleed A LOT. It kinda makes me sick to my stomach.

"Hey. Don't puke on the mattress," Evan says.

"I won't."

Caroline finally finishes and pours rubbing alcohol directly on it.

Evan or not, I yell. He laughs.

"It's done, little man," Evan announces. "Now you just got to take care of it."

I look down at a red, swollen mess of skin; I can't see the tattoo it-self. Evan smiles. "It takes a couple of weeks." He peers closely. "She did good, don't worry about it."

The beers wear off. I get home and rummage through Mom's bath-room cabinet for anything that might help, but she's either hidden it all or used it up. I dab on the alcohol like I'm supposed to, get woozy from the pain. I can't get near the liquor cabinet when my parents are home, so I take a bunch of aspirin. Dinner comes, and I somehow manage to shovel in food without anyone noticing that every time I move, I catch my breath. It's like razorblades slicing.

Dad's actually in a good mood tonight—everybody at work saw the article and now he's a big shot. Even Mom's into the conversation about justice and how sometimes good guys do win, and all that crap. Carl keeps glancing at me. Oh, now he wants to be my friend? Like I could do anything? I ignore him. After dinner, I escape to my room, pleading homework. A few minutes later, Carl comes in.

"Okay. What's wrong?" he asks.

"Nothing." I won't cry to my brother. He'll just tell his friends.

"Bullshit. You look dead, like when that car hit you. Remember? Remember that?"

"No, really? I got hit by a car? Wow. I forgot." I make a face at him. I have a fricking metal pin in my hip, what does he think? He opens my window and lights a cigarette, blows the smoke outside. "Do that in your own room." I want him gone; I need to lie down.

He holds out the cigarette pack. "Want one?"

"I don't smoke."

"Yeah you do. You also get pretty busy in the liquor cabinet."

How did he know? "What do you want, anyway?"

"Nothing. Can't a guy hang out with his brother?"

"You must want something."

"Why are you so weird tonight?" He puts the cigarette out on the windowsill, tucks the butt of it in his pocket.

"I got a tattoo, okay? It hurts."

His whole face changes. "My little brother, damn. Show me." I lift my shirt to show; I've already undone my pants.

"Is it a '13'?" He peers close. "I got one of those." He grins at me. "Who did yours?"

"Caroline Tuttle."

"Not bad. It's not too clear yet, but it'll probably get better."

"Sure as hell hope so."

"Got anything for it?" When I shake my head no, he winks. "I do. Bourbon and Coke. You bring the Coke."

I go downstairs for a couple of cans. Mom and Dad are so busy talking about Carl they barely notice me. I go to my brother's room. His black light's on and Jimi Hendrix looks amazing. He puts on "Purple Haze" and gulps down half of one of the Cokes. He fills the can with bourbon, sloshes it around.

"Check it out," he says, handing it to me and fixing one for himself. It burns going down, but that's okay. I like being here. I drink more. We shoot the shit. I tell him about Evelyn Anderson's tits.

"Yeah? Wait till you hear about Lucy," he says, taking a gulp of his own drink, then proceeds to give me a blow-by-blow of this girl he just slept with. My brother is so cool.

Sometime later, he walks me upstairs to my room. Good thing too, I'm pretty wobbly. Lying down on my bed is the last thing I remember until morning.

I survived that night because I didn't yet understand
about love or families or how life is supposed to go.
Or maybe I survived so I could tell my story. Whatever,
Doug's right—apologies don't change things.

# 1975

FIVE YEARS BEFORE

SAN FRANCISCO BAY AREA, CALIFORNIA

{1}

I'm dreaming I'm on the back of Dad's chopper, zooming down the highway with a bunch of his Hells Angels buddies, doing just fine until the cops start chasing us. They get closer and closer and their sirens get louder and louder. I'm getting scared until I wake up and find out it's not a dream at all. The sirens are here, at our house. Two fire trucks and an ambulance are in our yard, flashing red and yellow lights on the trees and Grandma and Grandpa's little back house. Firemen are un-hooking hoses.

I scramble down the stairs. Everybody's in the living room already. The front door's open; Mom and Dad stand there as a fireman comes up on our porch.

"Where's the fire?" he asks, his face turning red, then yellow, then red.

"There's no fire," Dad says. "Not here." Mom peeks around him, holding her robe closed tight at her neck.

"Uh, let's see —" The fireman glances at his notepad, looks at my mom. "Are you Mrs. Cooder?"

"Oh dear God," Mom says; Cooder's her maiden name. She pushes past Dad and runs between the trucks to Grandma and Grandpa's house. Dad follows with the firemen. All five of us kids huddle in a clump on the grass to see what's going on.

Grandma stands on her porch, white wispy hair sticking out of long braids, her robe flying open, flapping her arms wildly. She doesn't look like herself. I take Marianne's hand.

"I smell it, I smell it! The fire! It's in the basement, it's gonna burn us all up!" Her eyes look scary and she won't stop screaming. Mom grabs her shoulders, tries to calm her down.

"We'll check, lady, we'll check," the fireman says. "Come out here, come into the yard."

Grandma keeps shrieking. "Where's my Bob? Get Bobby!" Does she mean Uncle Bobby? Did she forget he doesn't live here now?

"He's gone, Mama," our mom says. "Bobby's gone. You know that." The firemen storm into the house. Grandpa stands to the side, shaking his head.

"Get the hoses! Get the hoses!" Grandma cries. "It's going to burn us! Put it out! Go find Bobby! Where's my son?"

The firemen check the house, garage, backyard, even the houses next door and across the street. They wake up the entire neighborhood. Finally, they turn off their lights and pull their big trucks out of our yard.

Mom and Grandpa help Grandma back inside their little house, and we go to ours. Davy falls right to sleep. Kaitlyn too. Paul and Marianne stay up, huddled on the couch, talking too low for me to hear. I try to sit next to Marianne.

"Not now, okay?" she says.

Everything's weird. Paul won't look at me; he hides his face. I go into the kitchen for cereal. My dad's already there, sitting at the kitchen table, a bottle of whiskey and a glass. He smiles, pulls out a chair, and tilts the bottle like he's offering it. I know he's teasing, but I shake my head no.

"Cheerios or Sugar Pops?" he asks, getting me a bowl.

"Sugar Pops."

"Crazy night, huh?" He pours the cereal and hands me the milk carton. "Scare ya?"

"Nope. Just a bunch of old fire trucks," I say, sounding braver than I feel.

"Scared the shit outta me." He pours himself another glass of his whiskey. I chomp on my cereal.

"When's Mommy coming back?"

"Probably not tonight. I think she'll stay with Grandma," he says.

I nod, taking this in. Grandma was the scariest part. "Is Grandma all right?"

"Sure, she's fine. She just made a mistake." He sips his drink, watches me. I don't like his expression. I wish we were hanging out in the garage. "She made one helluva big mistake."

I chomp my Sugar Pops, pour in a few more. "Oh, you mean Uncle Bobby?"

"Why would you say that?" Now his voice is scary too.

"Because he moved," I explain. "And Grandma thought he was getting burned up."

"Did she?"

"Uh-huh."

"Well, that was silly, wasn't it?"

"Yeah."

He scratches the side of his head with his little finger, and suddenly I stop eating and stare, a huge grin growing on my face.

"Daddy — are you wearing a hairnet?"

He makes a funny face. "Hey now, don't be talking about my hairnet." He adjusts it slightly, patting both sides. "Cool hair like this does not come easy."

# {2}

Mom looks up from cooking to check on us playing cards at the kitchen table — all except Paul, who's never home for dinner anymore, and, of course, me, sitting in the corner. I catch her gaze and smile, but she doesn't smile back. She sweeps the zucchini into a pot, fills it with water, and turns to put it on the stove. The front door slams.

"Daddy's here!" Davy cries, running to greet him.

"What about Go Fish?" Kaitlyn whines. She slaps her cards down, folds her arms across her chest, makes a pouty face. Marianne shakes her head at her.

"Stop being such a baby."

"I'm not a baby!" Kaitlyn whines louder.

"Wipe your feet, Joe!" my mother yells.

"No Paul?" Dad asks as we settle in for dinner. He asks this every night now and Mom shoots him one of those grown-up "shhh" looks. He sighs and shakes his head. He gently pats his Elvis hairdo then reaches for the chicken-fried steak. I grab firsts on the Tater Tots and, for once, get more than Davy.

"Your hair's gonna fall right off your head, Dad," Marianne teases. "You used my whole can of spray!"

"And he wears a hair net!" I add, giggling.

"There is nothing wrong with hairspray or hairnets," he says, touching his hair again. Davy reaches for the last of the Tater Tots and almost drops the bowl when Dad farts.

He cuts a big one, like gunfire.

"Geez, Dad —" Davy says.

"Oh, Daddy, gross!" Kaitlyn says, and covers her face. I go out of control laughing. Mom shakes her head at him.

"Joe, please. You're setting a bad example."

"It's not me," Dad says, throwing his palms up. "It's that damn elephant."

"Daddy!" Kaitlyn frantically waves her hand in front of her nose.

"Shit. There he is again!"

"Where is he, Dad?" I ask.

"Under the table, of course." He shrugs and holds his hands out, palms up. "Don't know how he does it!"

After dinner, I follow Dad out to the shop where he paints the signs that go on the side of those huge eighteen-wheeler trucks. He's famous for this because he doesn't use a stencil — he designs his own. Truckers from all over California pull their big rigs into our driveway. They know him by name. Dad brings out the beers he keeps in the little fridge; I get to have a sip and help put the signs onto the side. He tells jokes. The truckers laugh. I laugh too, even when I don't get the punch line.

I try to get out here every night; it's my best time. I sit with Dad in the big double garage he turned into a workroom. Down one whole side is a long wooden table where he rolls the signs out. In the corner he has his easel for painting. He makes magical, glowing, velvet paintings. People buy these too. He did Elvis for Mom. She loves it. It's in their room, on the wall by their bed.

I have my own tall stool where I sit and watch. Right next to it is Dad's Harley; sometimes I climb up on that. Sometimes we don't talk at all. I just watch him sip beer and do his art. Sometimes he asks me questions.

"How's school?"

"Great."

"Yeah? How you doing in history?"

"Pretty goddamn good."

"Watch your mouth now. Don't let Mom catch you cussing."

"I sure as hell won't."

He glances over and shakes his head a little, then laughs. "Chip off the old block, huh?"

"Damn straight." I get a grin a mile wide.

When he's done with the sign, Dad sets up his easel, then pulls out the smaller one he got just for me. He hums Roger Miller's "King of the Road." I chime in at the end: *"Ain't got no cigarettes!"* He puts a fresh canvas on mine and cocks his head in my direction.

"Want to do another dog?" he asks. I nod and he sketches it out, rolls over a cart with paints. He goes to his painting and I start mine. These are my best times and I know I will never ever forget them. My dad's the best.

## {3}

Paul doesn't come home that night or the next, and the day after that, Mom calls the cops. It takes them two weeks, but they find him, over in Oakland with Aunt Dora, my father's sister, and a bunch of her Hells Angels friends.

"Go get your father," Mom tells Marianne when two cops show up with Paul. He stares at the ground, arms crossed over his chest, looking mad. Dad comes up from his workshop. He's mad too. Me, Kait, and Davy get sent to our rooms; Marianne's almost Paul's age, so she's allowed to stay. We try to hear what's going on, but Mom sees us peeking and closes the door. They go out to the yard to talk. Ten minutes later, Paul's gone, in the car with the cops, Marianne's crying, and Mom closes herself up in her room. Dad heads back to his workshop without saying a word.

*      *      *

Aunt Dora and her husband roar into the yard an hour later, two of their friends trailing. They swerve and park their choppers in a row. Me and Davy go running out to meet them, but stop short when Dad gets there first. We stand very still and hope we won't be noticed. We need to find out what's happened to Paul.

"What the hell did you think you were doing?" Dad says. "You should've called us."

"He didn't want me to," Aunt Dora says.

"He's my kid, Dora. You shoulda let us know."

Mom comes out of the front door and across the yard. She's in her yellow dress and has her black hair curled and tied back. My aunt's wild red hair flutters in the wind. Her leather jacket flops open. I think of all the Christmases the two of them hung out and laughed together.

"You need to go, Dora," Mom says.

"I want to see Paul. I want to be sure he's okay."

"He's not here."

"Where is he then?"

"That's none of your business," Dad says.

"Go," Mom says. "I don't want to call the cops again."

"Fine." She gets on the back of her husband's bike. "But you can't just pretend it didn't happen. It happened, okay. You can't blame Paul for it either, or —"

My parents' heads snap to me and my brother.

"Shut up, Dora," Dad says.

"You kids go inside," my mom says. "Help your sister clean up the kitchen."

# 1976

## FOUR YEARS BEFORE

## LOS ANGELES COUNTY

Dad has to stand to cut the turkey. He stabs it with a huge fork and picks up a knife that reminds me of a miniature machete. I'm fascinated, can't look away. First the brown skin crinkles, then it splits. The blade saws through that thick white flesh, back and forth, down to the plate. He lifts the slice between the fork and knife and a piece of bird, which just a few weeks ago was running around, drops onto the plate. I like the sound of it. I love the smell. Chelsea pokes me and shakes her head. I shrug.

Hey. It's Thanksgiving.

Mom fills the plates, Dad's first, and sets them down in front of us. Chels chats about her new job at the dry cleaners and how they're training her to be a manager. She does not mention her boyfriend, Gabe. Mom and Dad don't like him. I think it's because he's big, and older. If my dad called *him* stupid, Gabe'd probably punch him out. I love listening to Chelsea, the way she talks about nothing and makes it sound good. It's nice having her back. I catch Carl's eyes—he too is wasted.

Mom starts grace and I wonder if the guy who shot Carl is eating turkey someplace. He jumped bail, which he should not have had in the first place. Dad was right about that.

"We thank thee for the bounty we are about to receive. Amen."

I add my own silent thanks for the killer pot Glenn shared with me an hour ago and wonder what Carl's on. We haven't been hanging out much lately, but me and him sure as shit know how to do a family dinner. He catches my eye and winks.

So far it's been great—Dad hasn't said a word. Maybe because Grandpa's not here to argue with? Usually, they'd be screaming by now, but Grams has a cold. Bad for her, good for us. Carl picks up his fork. I ask for the gravy.

"Did I tell you Mrs. Burch came in the other day?" Mom chats with Chelsea. As she hands me the gravy bowl, I get a flash of her bright, real smile. She loves having her whole family here. I expect she also loves not having *his*. "Remember her, Chels, your second grade—"

Mom stops mid-sentence to stare at Dad, who seems to have turned to stone. The image of a white cloud rising up out of his head comes to my mind, spreading into a mushroom shape over the table—like in those World War II newsreels we watch at school.

"How many times do I need to say it?" His voice is pitched low but manages to sound like a shout. "Potatoes go on the left, *Dumbass*. Meat on the right. How hard is that?"

Mom's face flushes. Her "sorry" gets pulled into the firestorm he always seems to create. Mom reaches to turn his plate, but not in time. He sweeps his arm across the table and everything in its path flies into the air. It all stays suspended for a blink, at least to my eyes, then crashes to the tile floor. Chelsea startles. Glasses shatter, yams splat, cranberries roll, silverware bounces.

If I wasn't stoned, I'd be scared. But I am, so I feel like laughing. Chels puts a hand on my arm. I look to see if Carl thinks it's funny too. He doesn't. His lips tighten and two bright points of color appear on his cheeks. Very deliberately, he sets down his fork as Mom darts into the kitchen for a new plate. She places it carefully—potatoes on the left, turkey on the right.

"Now was that too hard for you?"

The sarcasm in his voice makes my skin chill. He picks up his new fork and knife, like nothing happened, and begins to cut his turkey. My fork's in my hand but my plate's in the heap on the floor. Chelsea angles hers toward me and I spear a bite of turkey, but have no saliva to chew it. Dad looms over the table, slurping up mashed potatoes and guzzling beer.

No one mentions the mess.

"Anyway," Mom says, that other smile in place, "Mrs. Burch—"

Carl pushes back from the table and stands. "You're a jerk, man, you're an ignorant, stupid *jerk*." His voice is shrill and his body shakes. He holds his fists clenched at his sides. Chelsea stands, but so does Dad, so she sinks back down. This time I reach my hand to hers.

Like a snake striking, Dad snatches Carl's arm, swings him about and propels him backwards into the dining room wall. The force of it knocks Mom's painting onto the floor. Chelsea screams "Stop it!" and Carl jumps back, his face beet red. He shoves Dad with both hands and then swings his right arm and *lands a punch.*

Code Red.

Carl's never hit back before. Argued, yes, yelled, for sure—but never hit back. Dad's face scares me. He shifts to high speed. The two whirl about like Tasmanian Devils, knocking lamps and framed pictures off tables, the tiny antique mirror off the wall. Chelsea goes for the phone. Mom pleads. I watch.

My father beats my brother to the floor, *literally*, raises his gigantic leg and stomps down hard on his thigh. Carl bounces, grunts, then rolls away, balled up, arms curved over his face and head.

"Stupid asshole! Think you're big enough now? Do ya? Huh? Stupid shit!" Dad punctuates with kicks.

Carl's in the corner now; he can't escape. Mom clutches at Dad's arm; he hurls her backwards, then raises his hand to hit Carl again. I grab that arm from behind; he throws me practically into the hallway. I land on my bad hip and cry out. This stops everyone for a second, and all heads turn to me. Carl scrambles up and bolts through the front door, face and shirt covered in blood. His motorcycle roars to life and then he's gone.

Chelsea appears from the hallway, eyes blazing. "The police are on their way," she announces, placing herself between Dad and me. He takes a step toward her, hands still balled into fists.

"Do it. Please." Chelsea says, her voice as deep as a man's. "Hit me! Then you can hit Mom, or maybe Doug, huh, he's twelve. We'll get you locked up for the rest of your stupid life!"

For a second, it looks like he might. Time stops. In the far distance, a siren sounds. Mom sniffles. A lump rises on my cheekbone, where I hit the corner of the doorway, and the pain in my bad hip grows steadily worse. Dad snatches his keys and jacket and heads out the door, slamming it behind him. Mom turns immediately to Chelsea.

"Call them back, Chels," she says. "Quick! Tell them it was a mistake. We can't have police showing up here. The neighbors—"

"I didn't really call, Mom. I'm not stupid."

"Oh," Mom says, and touches her hair. "Of course you didn't, honey. I'm sorry." Her shoulders slump. "I'm so sorry."

Chelsea helps Mom clean up. She makes me put ice on my hip. We don't talk about Dad or Carl. We don't talk at all. After, Chels hugs us both and leaves. Mom pours a drink and takes it to her bedroom to watch TV. I listen for her to settle in, then look behind the fancy dishes in the kitchen cabinet, where Mom kept the Darvon she got when her finger was broken.

No luck. The bottle's not even there. No bourbon and Coke, either, so I pour a tall glass of orange juice and vodka. I grab a piece of turkey from Dad's plate and head up to my room. I don't want to be downstairs when he comes home. *If* he comes home. Sometimes he doesn't.

Carl's right—our father is a jerk. Who we put up with. Why do we do that? Why do we all keep trying so hard to make him happy? I can't remember a time when he was. He's always yelling at somebody, calling something stupid, just like his father. Grandpa's always yelling too.

I down a third of my drink and search for the roach Glenn let me have. I can't find it. With almost half the drink gone, my head fuzzes up but my hip still hurts. I try different positions. It doesn't help. It'd serve me right if this sucker hurt forever. I got it trying to please my dad.

When I was six, he yanked the training wheels off my two-wheeler. "Time to ride on your own, Doug," he announced.

"But I don't know how!"

"Sure you do. Every other kid on the block is riding." He held the bike out toward me. "Except you. We can't have that, can we?" I climbed on, the pit of my stomach in knots. He started to run down the street, pushing me from behind. I pedaled like crazy to keep up.

"Don't let go! Don't let go!" I screamed.

"Don't worry! I got ya!" he yelled back, shoved hard, and let go. The bike went a few more yards, then wobbled and crashed in the middle of the street. I landed on my elbows and knees. I tried not to cry but I couldn't help it. Mom raced out to help me and he stood there, shaking his head—I can still see his face—then picked up the bike and hung it on hooks in the garage.

So what'd I do? I practiced in secret. I had to prove to my dad that

I could do it. I practiced at Henry's, when he used to live here, and finally, *finally*, I got it. I couldn't wait to show Dad. I rode round and round on Henry's cul-de-sac street, feeling the power. Waiting for my dad to come around the corner and see me—and be proud.

"Doug! Look out!" was the last thing I remember before I bumped over the barrier and the world turned orange. I woke up in the hospital. My pelvis was cracked, the top of my hip broken. An old lady in an orange BMW had knocked me half a block. They put in a metal pin and slapped me in a body cast. No more sports. No more running. No more bikes.

My father laughed at first. He saw a lawsuit there. He got a lawyer. He spent a lot of money, but the court still said it was my fault. I shouldn't have been in the street.

Stupid. Once again.

I hear the front door downstairs. I take a gulp of my drink. I hear his car keys drop in the metal plate on the side table. The refrigerator door opens, a beer can pops. I chug the rest of my screwdriver and the room spins. Good for me. The pain may not go away, but I'll be asleep, so who cares?

# 1976

FOUR YEARS BEFORE

SAN FRANCISCO BAY AREA

All of a sudden, we're moving.

No warning that I know of; nobody talks about it. One Saturday morning, Mom tells us to pack up our stuff in the cardboard boxes she got from Safeway. We fill up the back of her car and drive everything over to a house on North Charlotte Street. Not too far from our real house. We make a whole bunch of trips and when the new place is filled up with boxes, she lets us order pizza for dinner. Sunday, we move our beds and some of the furniture. Dad helps, but I notice he doesn't talk much. Monday, we start a new school, a *Catholic* school, where we have to wear uniforms.

I keep waiting for my dad, but he never shows up.

I find out from hearing my mom on the phone that he won't be, ever. My parents are getting a divorce.

Paul doesn't come back. Marianne finally tells me and Davy that he got sent to Juvie, the same day the cops brought him home. She doesn't know which one, or who exactly it was that sent him; she suspects Dad. She thinks it's why Mom wanted to move.

"Why? What'd Paul do?" I ask her.

"Nothing. Ran away. I don't know. Maybe they got tired of him."

"You can't do that. You can't send your kid away for no good reason," Davy says.

"Obviously, you can."

"But why? Why would they do that?" I say.

"Stop asking me questions."

Dad gets the old house because that's where his work is done. He needs to keep working because Mom doesn't have a job yet, and now he has to support two houses. He's less than a mile away from us, but we're not allowed to visit. We're not allowed to do anything anymore. Mom has a ton of new rules. We have to come straight home after school. Me and Davy can go to our dance classes and Kaitlyn can go play on her softball team, but that's it. We can't have friends over when Mom's not home, and even when she is, she has to know all about their parents first. We are definitely not allowed to go to other people's houses.

Mom starts going to church a lot, and we have to go with her. We used to go every once in a while on Sundays; now it's every week. On Wednesday nights, we all go to the convent. We sit in a little room and help old nuns fix up clothes and toys for poor people. The nuns love our mom. They like Davy too, and Kaitlyn, because she never talks. They don't much like me or Marianne, but that's okay, because we don't much like them either. Especially not the ones who teach at the school.

I hate my new school. I don't mind the uniforms, but I hate the kids. I hate the new house even more. North Charlotte's a four-lane street and we don't even have a fence. You always hear traffic out front. There's a stop sign right at the corner, and all night, big old trucks grind their gears down and then start them up again. It makes me miss my dad even more.

Davy doesn't seem to mind being here, but Kaitlyn pretty much stops talking. She stands around looking at things. It's weird. Marianne keeps busy, and, as usual, I hang out by myself. I start really looking forward to Saturdays — going to dance class is the only thing I can count on. When I'm there, at the studio, I pretend nothing's changed.

We hardly ever see Grandma and Grandpa, and we all act like we never had a brother named Paul. Mom talks to us about right and wrong. She quotes the Bible, all the time.

Marianne says we traded Dad for God. I think she's right.

# Early 1977

THREE YEARS BEFORE

LOS ANGELES COUNTY

"Get me high, dude," I say to Roy. "Get me high."

I like saying that. I like how that sounds. It reminds me of Carl. I also like getting high. The older I get, the more it seems I need to stop my brain from over-thinking. I over-think a lot, which drives me batty. Sometimes I write poetry about it. I don't tell anybody because they'd probably laugh. Sometimes, drinking or smoking is just easier than sitting in my room writing down how bad I feel.

Anyway, it's Friday.

Friday, me and Roy like to hang out at the trailer park where he lives with his dad. It's way the hell out and I'm not supposed to be here.

"I already told you," Roy says, "I ain't got nothing."

"Where's your old man, dude? He'd buy."

"I don't know. Out."

"Come on, Roy."

"Well, I know this one guy . . ."

"Let's do it, man. Let's go."

\* \* \*

I made the mistake once of bringing Roy home. He stayed for dinner.
He was polite; he even made conversation with my parents. When he
left, Mom told me I'd "better not" see him again.

"Why not?"

"He's not like us, Doug."

"What's wrong with him? He's white."

"Don't sass your mother," Dad grunted.

"He's trash, Doug." Mom sighed like I was somehow mentally im-
paired. "He's not our people."

*Yeah, right, who is?*

It's just me at home now. Carl never came back after Thanksgiving.
I had to sneak his stuff out to him. He stayed with Chels and her boyfriend for a while, then moved in with some hippies in Hollywood—great, huh? Just when we were starting to get tight. My dad
tried calling the cops to bring him back, but Carl's over eighteen, so
no go. The best part was when the black guy got caught again and Carl
refused to testify. He dropped the charges. He made sure Chels told
my parents.

"What's wrong with that boy?" my dad raged, stomping back and
forth through the living room. Mom didn't say a word. She'd probably
figured it out, like me and Chels did. Nobody walks up to a car they
don't know in the middle of the night unless they're buying or selling
something. Carl and his buddies weren't as innocent as he pretended.

The guy Roy knows lives in a motel that looks like Dorothy's house after it dropped out of the tornado. Lots of blacks around too, dealing
drugs, hanging out with their skanky chicks. Who knows what *they're*
doing.

"Watch your mouth," Roy advises, then changes up his walk. I do
too. "Whatever you do, don't look scared."

He knocks on a door in the very back corner of the motel. A short dark-skinned guy opens it. Mexican. Greasy hair sticks to both sides of his face. He stares first at me, blinks and takes in Roy, then turns around. We follow him in. The room smells of pee and bleach, with some kind of rank incense burning in the corner that makes my eyes water. Off-key music blasts from a stereo perched on an orange crate. The guy squints at us, eyelids half shut. The drapes are drawn. He doesn't say his name.

"Hell no," he tells us, "I don't go buy no booze." He's got such a strong Spanish accent, I can barely understand him. "But I got NEB onna match head, *'migo,* you want some of that?"

"What's NEB?" I whisper to Roy.

"Connebenol," Roy says. "You'll like it." He nods at the guy. "How much?"

"What you got?"

Roy forks over ten. Poor as he is, he's always got cash for drugs. The guy scrapes yellow goopy shit off the end of the match onto a hand mirror, then chops it with a razor, leaving a wet film on the glass. He snorts some up through a little straw and hands the whole thing to Roy. Roy snorts and passes it to me.

"Don't take too much or your ears gonna fall off," the guy warns, then laughs, sounding like an old car starting up. I put the straw to my nose and snort.

A second later—a damn popcorn popper explodes inside my head! My jaw drops, all by itself; I can't close it. I drool like a stupid baby. My arms and legs go numb. I crumple back onto the couch, feel sweat trickle down both my sides. I see Roy at my side, in the exact same state. The Mexican guy's not shitting us. I can't move at all.

It's *completely* scary.

It's completely *amazing.* I catch one more glimpse of Roy then nod off.

*     *     *

I'm rolled from the couch and onto my feet. I'm not sure where I am or what the hell's happening until I see Roy, up and wobbly too. Right. NEB. The Mexican guy. How long have we been here?

"Time to go, *mijos*," he says, and pushes us gently toward the door. In the parking lot, there are only black faces, seems like everywhere, staring with dead fish eyes, talking shit. One of them laughs and shakes his head, reminding me of my dad. Weird. Somebody grabs my arm and I almost shit my pants until I see it's Roy.

"C'mon." We stumble over by a concrete wall, slump down behind a dumpster. "I can't walk yet, dude," he says. Me either. We hide there as the drug slowly wears off and feeling creeps back.

Something hard lands against the dumpster. A girl cries out. Roy puts his finger up to his lips and I nod. I may be wasted but I'm not about to call attention to us.

"Bitch. I tol' you 'bout that shit," a black guy says, and slaps her. She cries out again. He says something I can't hear, she starts crying and then her high heels click away. He lights a cigarette, inhales, follows the girl, boots clunking on the cement.

"Damn," I whisper.

"No shit," Roy agrees. Nobody should hit a girl. Even a black one.

"Dude. What time is it, man?" I ask a few minutes later.

"Why? You got something you gotta do?"

This strikes me as hysterically funny. "No, man, I got nothing to do. Not a damn thing."

*       *       *

Until two nights later.

It's late. I'm home, downstairs, watching TV; my parents have already gone to bed. I've fixed myself a screwdriver and swiped another pack of my mom's Pall Malls. Why they never notice this is beyond me. I used to try to hide it, pour water into the vodka bottles or Coke into bourbon, but why bother? Maybe they figure they already raised the two kids they planned to have. Or maybe they just don't care. I hold my history book, which I've not read, and click through channels until I find Don Kirshner's Rock Concert.

*"Easy like Sunday morning . . ."*

I scowl at the TV. Even homework's better than the Commodores. I find the chapter we're supposed to be reading and manage to drown the music out until Kirshner shows up and announces the next group.

"Ladies and gentlemen, welcome the Ramones!"

I don't look up until a chord sounds. Damn.

*What is this?*

Guys with long hair, tight jeans, clothes all ripped up, looking like skinny bikers, like they don't give a damn about anything. One guy stands taller and skinnier than me even, with a Dutch-boy haircut, a bowl cut. I can't take my eyes off him. He holds his guitar real low, plays his music with legs spread wide. Every once in a while he screams out "1, 2, 3, 4," in *German*.

*Who are these people?*

*"They are forming a straight line!"*

I set down my drink and reach for a cigarette, never shifting my eyes from the television.

*"These kids are losing their minds!"*

"Let's hear it for the Ramones!" Kirshner shouts.

*The Ramones.*

I try the name out loud. "The Ramones."

Singing directly to me.


"It's *Punk Rock*, man," Roy says the next day. "Where you been?" We're at Glenn's house. I'm playing them "Rocket to Russia," which I just discovered.

"I know it's Punk Rock, asshole," I say. "It's just, I didn't get it until last night."

"What's to get?" Roy mumbles.

"Yeah, well, if you like *them*, you need to check out the Sex Pistols," Glenn says. He always thinks he knows everything. He shoves in a new tape before I can say a word.

*I am an anti-Christ, I am an anarchist,*
*Don't know what I want, but I know how to get it . . ."*

"They're twice as good live." Glenn says, handing me the roach clip. He picks at one of his nasty zits. "I saw 'em in Frisco, at Winterland."

"Like hell you did," Roy says. I light the roach, suck at it, burn my lip, and pass it to Roy.

"I did," Glenn says. "Sid Vicious, man. Johnny Rotten. Outrageous, dude." He starts rolling a new joint. "They punched out the audience, man. Punched 'em out! You shoulda seen it. You shoulda seen that audience, man — safety pins stuck in their cheeks, through their eyebrows. Rings through their noses." He lights it, takes a drag, shakes his head, remembering. "Sid Vicious *jumped off* the stage, Doug, right on top of the crowd! Still singing!" He hands me the joint. "People wore dog collars, man. Chicks walked around with leashes on."

"I got to see this shit, man," I say, inhaling. I feel the truth of it deep inside me. "I got to see this shit."

# 1977

## THREE YEARS BEFORE

## SAN FRANCISCO BAY AREA

### {1}

God, his eyes are blue.

Even from across the studio, they glow; I can't look away. He tosses his dance bag to the corner, grabs the barre with both hands, and leans into it, stretching one amazingly muscular calf, then the other. Black hair, black dance pants, black wifebeater, the best butt in the world — Jonathan Grant, the most gorgeous boy in our class. In the whole San Francisco Dance Academy, for that matter.

Does Davy know I'm watching him?

Do I care?

My body tingles. I stumble over the legs of a girl stretching nearby, mumble sorry, and wonder how the hell I'm going to do ballet feeling like this. He glances my way, catches me staring, and smiles.

*Jonathan Grant smiles.*

At me, just turned twelve and small for my age — *me*, the mouse in the corner, okay but not great, nothing special, one of many. Until right now, this minute. Because not only does he smile — he walks toward me. I grab the barre and try to pretend a second position grande plié — but too late. He knows. My cheeks burn.

"Hey." His voice snakes inside my skin, wiggles up my spine.

"Hey," I croak. We've talked a couple of times the past few weeks, about classes or the *Nutcracker* auditions mostly, nothing personal. Someone always interrupted — older girls especially cannot keep away from this boy. He glances in the direction of the double-door storage room, back at me, and — if this is even possible — his eyes get bluer. He smiles, a different smile, an I-like-you smile, and mouths, "After class?"

I nod, just once because otherwise I'll have to scream out loud to everyone that Jonathan Grant wants to meet me after class. Not some stupid older interrupting girl — *me*.

I can't breathe right for a few seconds and hope like hell Davy isn't looking. Jonathan strolls to his usual place at the barre just as Madame Nevonski enters, gray hair tight in a bun and skirt swirling. She taps her cane twice on the floor.

"Class. To the barre."

I love her raspy smoker's voice, which reminds me of my aunt Dora, and her thick Russian accent. She demonstrates with arms only, then taps the cane again and eases her plump self onto the tall stool near the piano. It's hard to believe she's one of those amazingly beautiful dancers pictured in the gallery in the hall.

The pianist begins. As one, thirty-five kids plié into our first of four Saturday classes. Davy's at the barre near Jonathan, competing with the better boy dancers, as usual, and being brilliant. As usual. Right now, I don't care if everybody thinks my big brother's the next Baryshnikov. Jonathan Grant and I are meeting in the storage room after class.

"What's wrong with you today?" Davy asks, when finally (finally!) the longest class I've ever taken ends.

"Nothing." I make a face at him. "What's wrong with you?"

"*You,*" he says, and makes a face back. I stick my tongue out. He wipes sweat from his forehead and the back of his neck, and from over by the piano, Isabelle Sanchez watches. She's almost sixteen. Not-quite-fourteen-year-old boys are not supposed to look like my brother does, manly and powerful with his square shoulders and muscles. Everybody likes him. Even Madame Nevonski, who smiles now and nods at him as she sashays her old dancer's body out of the room. Davy stares at me; he tilts his head the way he does when he's trying to figure something out.

"What? I got a cramp, okay?" I massage my calf.

"Davy!" Isabelle calls.

"Your girlfriend's calling," I tease.

"Shut up. She's not my girlfriend."

"Davy, are you coming?" She sings it.

"Tell *her* that," I say.

*        *        *

"Hey there, pretty," Jonathan whispers when I open the storage room door. My legs go weak. He peeks through a cloud of green and gold tulle painted for the Sugar Plum Fairy. I take a sharp deep breath; this is really happening. He holds out his hand; I wade through tutus and fabric to grab it. The skin where we touch warms instantly; I imagine it glowing, embers in a fireplace.

I step over a box of fairy wings and settle on the floor beside him. He slips his arm around me and scoots me closer. His eyes! — Jesus God — I can't quite catch my breath. He cups my face, more warmth and light where his palm caresses my cheek. He's breathing faster now too; his eyes melt, hazy and soft. I hear Ms. Marguerite's beginning ballet class start next door. Another world.

"I want to kiss you," he whispers. "Can I kiss you?" I nod — at least I think I do; I can't be sure of anything right now. He leans close, slides his hand down the back of my head. I put my arms around him. We kiss — my first kiss ever. His lips are soft, sooooo soft, his breath smells of mint, he has a faint musky odor from dancing; he's perfect. Being touched by him goes beyond words; the only one I can find is *grand*.

This feeling is *grand*.

"Oh my God," I whisper, my voice husky.

"Yeah," he replies, his voice husky too.

"Is it okay, I mean, that we — " I try to smile but the muscles don't seem to be working.

"Shhhhh. Yes. It's wonderful." He kisses my nose, then my lips, and pulls back to look at my face. "Oh my God, you have such beautiful eyes." He kisses me again. He whispers sweet words, touches my face, strokes my hair, kisses me more. I kiss him back. I've dreamed this, I've hoped it, but nothing I imagined was ever huge enough to describe how it actually feels.

Grand.

Like a first taste of air after someone's held your face underwater. Like falling off a cliff in a dream, and learning that you can fly.

I am *here*.

Like a window flung open, sharp fresh winter wind whipping through a closed-up, cluttered room, clearing it, making it new.

I am totally and absolutely *here*.

This is real.

This is me.

I note it, so that I can keep it. My body, my mind, and my heart are finally all in the same room.

Grand.

{2}

"Bless us, O Lord, and these Thy gifts which we are about to receive from Thy bounty . . ."

Davy stares across at me as Mom says grace. Under the table, he shoves Kaitlyn's chair with his feet, once — and getting no reaction — again. We all glare at him, just as Mom adds, "Amen."

She wears yellow tonight, her best color, a fitted shirtwaist dress I remember from last year's back-to-school night. Brushing a lock of hair back from her face, she picks up her fork, the signal that we can start eating. Her nails are crimson red, like a model's, fingers and toes. I used that exact nail polish one day last month when I stayed home from school. I had the house to myself. I did my feet, so no one would notice, but Mom came home early. I heard her car in the driveway and panicked. We're never supposed to go in her bedroom. I shoved my feet in socks, ruining all my work, and forgot to put the bottle away. Kaitlyn got blamed.

"Wake up!" Kaitlyn hisses at me now.

"Mom asked how was your day?" Marianne prompts.

"It was fine, thank you," I say, smiling. Jonathan Grant's blue eyes float through my mind and my cheeks get warm.

Davy tips his head that way. "How could it be fine?" he taunts. "You said you hurt your leg."

"I said I had a cramp," I said, shooting him a warning. Why is he always trying to start trouble? I knew things about him too. "But thanks for asking."

"Davy's a good boy," Mom says. Behind her back, Marianne rolls her eyes. Davy pretends he doesn't see. He's the favorite, but it's not his fault and we're all used to it. He's a prodigy; a dancer, like Mom used to be. He could do any dance you showed him from the time he could walk. Mom took him to San Francisco to study at the Conservatory, and a year later, sent me too. I think she was hoping I'd be a star like Davy, but I'm not. Still I liked it, especially the shows — getting costumes and doing makeup and going on tour. I love it now.

It's Davy's and my night to clear the table. Marianne and Kaitlyn wait in the living room. When we're done, Mom kneels to start. We kneel too. Jesus looks down on us. Jesus watches us everywhere we go in this room. He's the biggest statue and the first thing you see when you come in our new house. I have nightmares about His eyes following me.

"Hail Mary, full of grace, the Lord is with thee . . ."

"Our Father, who art in Heaven . . ."

We say our parts; Mom starts Thanks and Blessings. Davy hits Kaitlyn with a kernel of corn he stowed in his cheek. Kait sticks her tongue out and I squeeze my lips together to keep from laughing.

"O great and almighty God!" Mom prays on, "we kneel before You to thank You with our whole hearts for all the favors which You have bestowed upon us this day. . . .

Kaitlyn pokes Davy, who kicks his foot in her general direction and lands hard on her thigh.

"UNH!" she grunts. We all hold our breath —

". . . for all those other mercies, which we do not now recall . . ."

— but Mom doesn't hear. Davy spits another kernel; this one smacks Marianne dead on the cheek. My whole body is jiggling from holding in my laughter. Davy pushes Kaitlyn, she leans over onto me. Nobody falls, but the air's disturbed, movement ripples through. Suddenly, Mom stops praying and stands up, as still as ice.

"Shit," Marianne whispers.

"Excuse me?!?"

"Nothing, Mama. It slipped out. I'm very sorry, please forgive me?" Marianne says, her face absolutely blank. We're all good at "blank."

I hear a truck grind its gears to a stop at the corner light. I think of my father. The truck starts up. I wonder if it has a sign painted by my dad. If maybe I met the trucker one time, when he came to pick it up. We lower our hands and watch Mom pace slowly back and forth, searching our faces. We do not get off our knees. She doesn't look beautiful now. She looks mean, like she could do anything at all to us and not care. I hate the feeling in my stomach and the faces of my brother and sisters.

Dad's punishments were always a formula — three swats for cussing, six for fighting, more for the older kids, less for the younger, then it was done, over, forgotten. Mom adds them up, keeps track. We don't make mistakes, we commit sins. That sin attaches to the one before, and those before that, and as the list gets longer, each one of us kids gets closer to HELL. I wish they weren't divorced.

"Okay. Who started it?"

No one answers. Snitching's okay with small stuff like being late to class, but not this. This was interrupting evening prayers. If we give up Davy, we have to give up Kaitlyn and me, and Marianne. There's no telling what Mom might do.

"Last chance."

Silence.

"All right, then, on the wall. All of you." We stand, our knees imprinted with the pattern of the tile on the fireplace, and find a place along one of the living room walls.

"This is the Lord's house." She pauses, walks across the room like the Nazi guy on *Hogan's Heroes*. "Respect that or find somewhere else to live. Do you hear?"

"Yes, ma'am," we say as one.

"Good. Now pray that Jesus forgives you your sins."

I stand with my nose an inch away from the shades on the window that faces the street. Mom kneels by the fireplace, next to the statue of Jesus. Mother Mary's on the other side. This is her shrine: holy candles and small statues of saints perched on the mantel, a picture of each of us on the wall above, Jesus and Mary on the pavers in front. On a small table to the left is a tiny clear bowl, my mother's greatest prize, holy water brought from Lourdes by Father O'Malley, just for her.

Mom prays a Hail Mary and then asks for forgiveness. "Blessed Father, I know I have sinned." I wish she'd take her Jesus and go live in the church. We could go back to Dad's. Except then her voice changes and she starts to sound like a little lost girl, which makes me want to hug her and tell her it'll all be okay. But Jesus's eyes bore into the back of my head and I don't dare move.

I hate this feeling. I miss my dad. I blink back tears because I don't want to get laughed at by my brother. I focus on this morning and hiding in the storage room. I think of blue eyes and sweet kisses. I try to remember how it felt to be full and there and real.

"I have many crosses to bear," Mom prays. "Help me, Father, for I cannot bear them alone."

# {3}

Davy presses his transistor radio to his ear, closes his eyes, and lets his feet rehearse choreography. We're on BART, heading for San Francisco. We audition today for *The Nutcracker*; Mom's driving over later to watch.

Davy can do whole dances in his head, tapping his feet, twitching his body, practicing without even standing up. People can't tell what he's doing. They don't even notice, but he wouldn't care if they did. "Tough shit," he'd say. I like that about him. I wish I could stand up and be loud. I actually like my brother a lot; besides my dad, he's my best friend. We spend the most time together because of dance.

Now, as we head down through the tunnel that goes under the Bay, just in that moment of darkness before the tunnel light flickers on, I smile — because I have my brother, because it's Saturday, and mostly because now, boys like me. Some kind of secret beacon switched on in me after Jonathan. Boys who never even glanced my way now speak as we pass in the halls; boys who'd ignored me in class send messages with their eyes across the studio as we work at the barre. Boys I admired but never talked to sit with me to chat at break. I don't even care that Jon likes someone else now. Michael likes me, and he's even cuter.

I live for Saturdays. It's what I think about when Hugo Leone and Ralph Conifer make me climb behind the lockers in the seventh grade hall and wait there until they leave. This started the first day we went to St. Anne's. I never did anything to them.

"You get outta there before we're gone, you know what happens," fat Ralph Conifer says.

"We put the trash in the garbage can!" Hugo Leone chants. "Oh yeah, we put the trash in the garbage can."

I know they will, they've done it.

"You gotta fight back," Marianne told me once when she came to pick me up and I was brushing the junk off my school uniform. "You got to stand up for yourself. They're just bullies."

I think it's easier to put up with it. They don't really hurt me, but they might if I argued back. If I call Dad, he'll talk to their parents and who knows how bad it could get then. Mom would report it to Sister Mary Margaret, and Sister likes them way better than she likes me. I get on her nerves, I can tell that by how her face tightens when I come into English. Besides, if I tell Mom, Marianne will get in trouble for not protecting me. So I just put up with it and wait for Saturday.

Two things happen in this audition. Teachers figure out who stays or moves up a level, and this year's cast for *The Nutcracker* is chosen.

Almost all the parts are already decided, but parents come anyway, to watch, hope, and cheer their kids on.

The crowd of mostly moms is packed into the viewing area at the end of the big studio, politely smiling and nervously pushing at each other to get nearer to the front. Except our mother. She stands out, partly because she looks absolutely stunning in her pink dress, mostly because she's the only one who isn't paying attention. She smokes a cigarette, reads her novel, and every once in a while glances toward us.

Davy tells me to go across the floor with him. Instead of doing the leaps and turns we're all supposed to, he wants us to walk, do a single châiné, and make a big ending pose. Kids bust into laughter. Davy winks at Madame Nevonski, who shakes her head at us — well, at him — and smiles. She adores him. We don't go across the second time.

Davy heads off with Isabelle and I go stand with a group of boys. I'm laughing at something Michael's saying when I notice Mom stomping toward me. She walks right into the studio and yanks me to one side.

"Don't you ever embarrass me like that again," she says. "Do NOT."

"But, we were just —"

"Are you talking back??"

"No, Mom, but Davy —" I want to say it's all right, it was planned, he knew we'd be cast anyway.

"I will deal with your brother separately. You are on restriction, do you understand?"

"Yes, ma'am." But I don't.

She might as well have slapped me. My face burns from shame and I don't even know what I did except follow her precious Davy.

I ditch afternoon classes. I'm not up to dancing or even hanging out with Michael; I go downtown. It's loud and dirty, filled with people who remind me of Jacques Cousteau's sharks circling around, looking for blood. Not what I need. Some other time, maybe, I'll come back and watch all the weirdos, but now, I have to think. I head up Market Street, past the Safeway. I figure I have three hours before Davy will look for me to go back home. I have money in my pocket to get lunch; I'll just find a good place to eat and this will all seem — I round a corner and freeze.

Am I still in San Francisco?

Or is this a movie set?

It has to be — nothing's this perfect. Everything on the entire street seems placed just so, clean and colorful. Trees decorate the sidewalks and skinny Victorians stand side by side like brightly painted little soldiers. Flower pots brighten restaurant windows. The air is clean, the street framed by a hint of fog.

But it isn't just that. It's the people.

They're beautiful. They walk together, holding hands, kissing, liking each other — right out in the open. Squeaky-clean faces in fresh clothes, strolling with arms linked, sitting at tables on the sidewalk, leaning in to smile at each other, holding hands over glasses of wine and tea, having conversations. Laughing. Listening. Everything lovely, normal, good.

No one gives me a second glance as I wander down the sidewalk to check it all out. I realize I've actually heard lots about Castro Street, but I never expected it would be like this: perfect, a separate magical little village. I want to live here. I want to be one of the beautiful people who talk to each other, smile and laugh and pat each other on the back. I want to go to the outdoor cafes, shop in the stores, sit on the benches, and look at the trees.

The afternoon flies by and too soon, I have to get back. I know I won't be able to stay away. Maybe I'll bring Michael here, or maybe I won't. Maybe I'll just save it for myself. I'll walk around. I won't talk to anyone, since I don't really live here, not yet, but I'll look. Listen. Soak up all the good energy and light. I'll try on clothes in the shop around the corner. I'll sit at an outdoor café and order tea. I'll move and sway to the music that floats out of the lounges. I'll sniff the cologne the guys are wearing. I'll tingle and laugh and feel grand.

## {4}

Davy got Fritz. Fritz is major. Fritz dances in the third act, and people who dance in the third act *get paid.* My mother cannot stop smiling. She's already called her friend Gladys and our grandparents.

"Be sure to tell Joe," she instructs Grandpa. "My son is the youngest dancer ever to get Fritz."

At dinner, the rest of us are expected to be happy for Davy, so we are. We congratulate him. We are impressed that he had his picture taken today for a newspaper article in the *Chronicle*. At some point, Marianne asks what I got.

"A soldier," I say and smile. "At least you'll see my face." Last year I was a mouse and the costume covered me completely. We skip evening prayers to go for ice cream. Mom orders a big bowl of five different flavors and we crowd into the booth in the back corner, each with our own spoon.

"Sit up!" she orders and we do. "Use your napkins." She smiles at my brother. "To Davy," she says, holding up a spoonful of Chocolate Mint. I hold up my French vanilla and smile. I hate Davy right now. It's so easy for him to be adored. I watch his every move and can never figure out what he does that makes her love him best.

In silence, we eat.

"Hey, Mom?" Kaitlyn blurts, "what did Uncle Bobby get arrested for?" We jerk our heads toward her; she barely talks these days.

"Don't, Kait," Marianne whispers.

Mom sits up straighter, if that's possible. "Don't be rude, Kaitlyn. We're celebrating Davy."

"I didn't know Uncle Bobby got arrested," I said.

"Shhh," Marianne says.

"Yeah, well, this girl at school is telling everybody he molested a bunch of kids." Kait pops her spoon in her mouth, speaks through green pistachio ice cream. "I just wanted to know if it's true."

"Keep it up, young lady," Mom says, standing, glaring at Kaitlyn. "You'll find yourself living with your father."

"I wish," Kait mutters; only I hear. The ice cream's not finished, but we're all standing up now, putting on our coats, going home. We don't talk all the way there. Davy pouts; he had a whole scoop left. I'm glad.

*　*　*

"I thought Uncle Bobby moved away," I say. Me and Marianne are sitting on the couch. She's doing her nails. Mom's talking on the phone in the kitchen. Kait was sent to her room. I have no idea where Davy is and I don't really care. I angle myself so Jesus can't see me.

"Nope. Arrested."

"For what? Smoking pot?"

She shoots me a funny look.

"Well, he didn't exactly hide it. Was that it?"

"Nope. Polaroids." She hands me the nail polish bottle. "Hold this." It's the same bright red as Mom's. I wonder if it is Mom's.

"Of what?"

"Naked kids. Gross, huh?"

"Did you see them?"

"No, but I heard. Daddy found a shoebox full."

"Shit."

"Yeah. Bummer, huh? Our uncle's a pervert." She dabs the brush in the bottle, starts on her other hand. "But then, Grandma's a nutcase. Remember how she called the fire department?" I nod. "Well, she kept calling them — for weeks. They took out a restraining order. Grandpa had to put a lock on the phone."

"Jesus." I glance at the statue, whisper "sorry."

"Yep. That's when Mom got religious." She stops painting to stare at me. Really stare.

"What?" I ask.

"Nothing, never mind."

"No. *What?*"

"Paul was in the pictures. So were you."

"I was not."

She goes back to her nails, like she's not listening.

"That's stupid, Marianne. Don't you think I'd know?"

"I guess, whatever." She dabs on her second coat, wipes a smudge with the side of her thumb.

I don't like the feeling in the pit of my stomach. "Why do you think that? You said you didn't see them."

"I heard Mom talking to the cops. And Paul told me some stuff." She waves her hands back and forth to dry her nails. "It's why he ran away, you know. Daddy yelled at him for letting it happen."

It's suddenly hard to breathe, like on the Halloween when I wore a nylon stocking over my head. I keep looking at my sister. I don't remember cops at our house, except the ones that brought Paul home. I sure as hell don't remember any Polaroids.

She blows on one finger, touches it gently to her lip to test if it's dry. "This family is so messed up." She takes back the polish bottle and screws the cap on, snags a cigarette from her purse, stares at me once more, chuckles. "All of us, we're crazy." She glances toward the kitchen, scoops up matches from the table. "Get me before she comes back in."

I nod and she slips out to the front porch. Jesus stares down at me and all of a sudden, I feel very small.

*       *       *

*The Nutcracker* goes up; Davy's amazing as usual. I do okay and I have a great time on the tour. Mom gives us each flowers on opening night. I get to miss two days of school when the show goes on tour. Nobody mentions Uncle Bobby again, not even Kait.

Christmas Eve, we have our usual procession. We dress up in robe costumes and march from the backyard to the front. We go from oldest to youngest, so Marianne's first, carrying Mary and Joseph, since Paul's not here. Davy has the cow and the lamb. I get stuck with the palm fronds. Kait's got Baby Jesus. Mom waits in front, by the empty cradle.

We've done this for years. It used to be fun.

"Everyone else puts the whole scene up at the same time, Lori," Dad would tease, back at the old house.

"Everyone else is wrong," Mom would say, laughing. "Mary didn't get there until after dark."

That's when we march. Except here, in the new house, we're on a busy street, not a secluded yard like before. "This is so embarrassing," Kait whispers.

"Shh, just get it over with," Marianne mumbles, as we go round to the front yard.

"I knew I shoulda burned the stupid statues," Davy whispers.

"They won't burn, dummy," Kait hisses.

A guy in a truck going by honks his horn. "What are you all supposed to be?" he yells out, then laughs.

Mom's lips tighten. I look back at Kait. She shakes her head slightly. Marianne stares at the ground. Davy's eyes have gone completely blank. Each of us takes our turn to place our pieces in their proper positions. Marianne sets down Mary and Joseph, Davy does the cow and the lamb, and I lay the palm fronds in the center of the cradle. Kaitlyn, eyes scary with anger, puts in the baby.

We stand in a line, clasp our fingers together, and bow our heads as our beautiful mother prays to a plastic Baby Jesus.

# Late 1977

## THREE YEARS BEFORE

### LOS ANGELES COUNTY

{1}

I start my band the summer before ninth grade. Glenn plays bass. I sing. Roy can't do shit but he's got his dad's guitar so we let him be the guitarist. Glenn shows him some chords and he learns to play them—real fast and real loud. This guy Craig has drums. I buy all the music I can afford: Black Flag, the Clash, Sex Pistols. More Punk Rock's coming out every day.

Finally! Something in the world that I can relate to. *Punk Rock*. It means: No rules. It's made for me and everybody else who doesn't fit in. I grow my hair like Johnny Ramone and start writing songs. Now all that poetry I used to do has a place to go. Words pour out of me. Everything that used to feel crazy makes sense. I make sense. I have a direction. I have my music. It's what I'm going to do with my life—be a Punk Rocker. Say something important. Make it big. I won't even have to graduate from high school.

It's wild.

I'm wild, getting wilder.

On Saturdays, the band rehearses inside an old elementary school that's been boarded up for years. We pry the wood off the back windows—it snaps easy, rotted. We drag in Craig's drums and set up in the multi-purpose room, which, for some reason, still has electricity. We can play as loud as we want; nobody is anywhere near around.

Our third time there, we decide to decorate. We spray paint obscenities all down on the walls in the main hallway, RAMONES and BLACK SABBATH on the blackboards in the kindergarten room. Glenn tries to spray paint a naked girl but he starts with the tits and it looks really stupid.

We work on our own songs and practice covers from any band we can think of. On our break, we drink the beers Roy scored from his dad. Glenn goes back to trying to spray paint tits. He's on his third pair when Roy interrupts him.

"Gimme that," Roy says, pointing to the can of spray paint.

"Just wait, I'm almost done," Glenn said. Roy snatches it anyway.

"What the hell are you doing?" I ask.

"Watch." Roy pulls a rag out of his pocket, sprays it and drops the whole thing into a plastic bag. He holds the bag over his mouth and nose, sucks in the fumes, and gets this shit-eating grin on his face.

"Oh man oh man oh man!" He holds out the bag.

I don't let myself even think; if Roy can do it, I can. I grab the spray paint and do exactly what he did. My mouth floods with a chemical taste then, BAM!! My heart jumps right out of my chest and I swear my whole brain slams into the back my skull.

"SHIT!" I manage.

"Yeah." Roy laughs. "Huffing, dude. Huffing. Punks do it all over in England."

"I want to," says Glenn. Roy sprays the shirt again. Glenn huffs. He whoops. We turn to Craig.

"Nah, that's okay."

"Chicken?" Roy says. Craig stares for a second, then slowly reaches for the bag. We watch as he huffs.

"Dude, that was bogus," I tell him. "Do it again."

"Nah, that's all right."

"Pussy," Glenn says. Craig shakes his head no.

"You can die from that shit, man. I saw it on a TV program."

"You can die from life, dude," I say, and huff again.

We start getting gigs! They aren't much, just some other bands that let us play a set at a yard party here and there. People have yard parties all the time now, all over the Inland Empire, down in Orange County, out in Venice. Punk Rock is coming into its own. It's not the Punk the British have; our Punks aren't poor. In America, it's the middle class that's messed up. Before Punk, we had nothing but greed and hypocrisy. Now we got a way to fight back, say who we are, stand out.

I start pegging my jeans real tight. I buy a plaid shirt from the Salvation Army and sneak my dad's engineer boots from the back of his closet. Kids at school try to make fun of me, but I don't even listen. I don't listen to anything I don't want to hear. I don't care that there's only one other Punk in my grade. This is not about popularity; I'm just being who I am. I'm tired of faking it. I'm tired of wasting time worrying about somebody else's bullshit. We're all gonna die sooner or later—more likely, sooner, so who cares? The world is in *chaos*. I know this. I don't need shit from anybody. I do my music. I make my own chances.

That's Punk.

Friday, as usual, I trek over to Roy's. Time for some R and R.

"Went up to see his mom," his dad tells me. "Chowchilla. It's her birthday."

"Oh. Thanks." I stand there hoping he'll at least offer me a beer, like usual, but when a woman pokes her head around the corner, he grins and closes the door.

Great. Here I am, all the way out at the stupid trailer park, needing to relax and no way to do it. My parents are home and Glenn's not available. What the hell am I supposed to do now? I truck over to the liquor store and wait to see if there might be somebody who'd buy. No luck. The only customers that come in look like they'd just steal my cash. Should I go to the motel? Alone? Stupid idea. But, hey, wouldn't be my first.

The Mexican guy waves me in. I pay, he lays out the NEB. I chop it myself, then snort, close my eyes, and sink down into the chair. What seems like seconds later, the guy calls out.

"Hey. Come rub my legs, *mijo*." He pats the couch cushion next to him. "I got bad pain."

"Your momma," I slur, nodding off.

"I give you free, today." I open my eyes; he's standing directly in front of me. He leans down and ruffles my hair. "One little rub, *mijo*."

I try to push myself up and out of the chair; he whirls me easily onto the couch, sits down beside me, takes my hand, and puts it on the front of his pants. I can't raise my arms to stop him. He leans in close; I gag at the smell. He moves my hand back and forth. Reaches for my zipper.

Adrenaline kicks in and suddenly I'm up. I knock the bastard on his ass. I book it out the door, stumble through the parking lot. I moving but I'm not sure how; I can't feel my legs or lower back. I crawl behind the dumpster to hide there until I come down enough to walk home. My head is splitting. What the hell am I doing here? I could have been raped. Not a white face in sight and I can't run. I'm on NEB. PCP. ANIMAL TRANQUILIZER.

Stupid doesn't begin to describe it.

"Hey, baby," says a black chick, leaning around the edge of the dumpster. Her eyes are glassy. "You want a date?"

"Fuck off." I manage to stand up, but that doesn't last. Some ugly black dude grabs my shirt and sends me flying into the gravel on the edge of the parking lot.

"Apologize to the lady," he says, his eyes boring into me. His buddies come up behind him. I'm so scared I pee my pants.

"Sorry," I mumble.

"Couldn't hear ya," he says.

"I'm very sorry," I say.

"Yeah you are," the guy says and they all start laughing. "You are one sorry mother—"

A cop car drives down the alley and slows, shining a light toward us. The group breaks up quick. I don't wait around.

When I meet up with Roy a couple days later, I tell him what the Mexican tried to do. I don't mention the other. He laughs.

"Shit, he tries that with everybody. You ain't special."

"Why didn't you tell me?"

"Why didn't you ask?"

I deck him. He laughs again.

## {2}

Here's what I figure out.

If I want to play music, I got to go out and hear people playing it, see how they perform, get into the scene. Punk Rock's taking off, moving like wildfire. It's a revolution. I can't sit around with Roy all the time. I can maybe drink and smoke some pot, but that NEB shit?

Taking those stupid chances? No more. I won't spend my life being unconscious. I got too much to say. Music is the way I'm gonna say it. Not hanging out with trash, being stoned.

I need to take charge of my life.

"You are so right," Glenn says, when I talk it over with him. "Roy ain't shit, man. He can't even play. We got to move forward, yeah? Check this out." He holds up a flyer for Black Flag, the one that's like the Manson girls. "Want to go?"

We don't tell our parents; we just go. Me and Glenn ride the bus more than an hour to get to Hollywood. We sit in the very back, him in his ripped-up shirt and jeans, me wearing my Ramones T-shirt. We put on our mean faces and like it a lot when this woman chooses to stand up rather than sit near us. We get off up by Highland and stroll down Sunset. Hollywood at night is way better than I ever imagined. The energy's like a drug. At the Whiskey, we stand in line with all those people I've been wanting to meet—the ones with dog collars and spiked hair. Glenn almost chickens out.

"Just shut up and look pissed," I whisper. We're both over six feet tall. We do not look fifteen. When the bouncer gives us the once over and nods toward the door, I want to scream out loud.

We're in!

Music blasts, lights strobe, people press close around us. The MC glares out at the crowd.

"Who let all you long hairs in here?" he rants into the microphone.

I know he can't be talking to me—my hair's like Johnny Ramone's. That's Punk.

"Don't you people know short hair is All-American?" he screams.

Somebody yanks my hair from behind, hard. I whirl to see a little round Punk girl smirking. Her head's shaved. She's got a safety pin stuck through her eyebrow.

"Hippie," she taunts.

"Bitch," I say. My hair is definitely not hippie.

A second later, I smell something burning. Glenn smacks the back of my head.

"She lit your hair, man," Glenn says and smacks me again.

I cuss the girl out and shove her backwards. She falls into her boyfriend, a big blond flattop wearing a collar with spikes. I didn't notice him. He pops me one, dead on, center of my forehead. My head whips back like a bobble doll. The girl laughs.

This is not what I expected.

Glenn presses through bodies and drags me away from them, somehow gets us closer to the stage; I'm dizzy and stink of burnt hair, with a bump rising in the center of my face. What the hell's different from that stupid motel? Everybody keeps trying to mess me up.

The MC rants on as the band sets up behind him. People jump on the stage; he kicks them back off. He punches one guy. Glenn slips me a flask and I gulp some whiskey. It burns going down. I'm about ready to suggest we get outta here when Black Flag kicks in.

*"I ain't got no friends to call my own!"*

Lights change colors. People scream out the lyrics. Somebody starts to pogo and in an instant, the entire room's jumping up and down, as one, including us. Everything starts to blur. The music's going faster than my heart, but I'm catching up. The pounding in my head is now coming from the stage, and I can't tell where I stop and everybody else begins. Long hair, short or shaved, we're all Punk now—one mind, one single body. Nothing else exists. Dez Cadena catapults off the stage and onto the crowd. People carry him over their heads. I reach up and feel his weight as he travels across the room, never dropping the mic from his mouth:

*"Depression's gonna kill me!"*

# Early 1978

TWO YEARS BEFORE

SAN FRANCISCO BAY AREA

{1}

Sometimes on Sundays, I pretend to have a headache so I won't have to go to church. Marianne knows I'm faking, but doesn't say anything. We take care of each other.

Today, I lounge in the old iron chair on the front porch; it's got a big round spring so you can rock back and forth, side to side, or even in a circle. I like how it creaks. I think about my family. I wonder about my dad, if he's out in the garage doing a sign. I wonder if Paul's okay. When he turned eighteen, he got out of Juvie and decided not to come back home.

"Your brother broke my heart," Mom said when she found out. "Every time the phone rings at night, I know it will be something bad. I couldn't live if anything happened to one of you kids."

I wonder if that's true.

I creak the chair around. I like how it feels. I like being where I'm not supposed to be. I start counting the cars that whiz by, trying to keep track of how many I see of each color. The street's busy this morning — it adds up fast.

A bright yellow van goes by, the color of a school bus. It's number three on yellows. A baby blue Bug is twelve, or maybe thirteen of blues. Another red car is twenty-one. One more yellow van — no, wait, it's the same one. Should I count it twice? Why not? Four yellows. Five minutes later, it comes by again. I sit up. The guy driving pulls over to the curb and beckons me over.

"I'm afraid I'm lost," he calls out, smiling, very friendly. I walk down the sidewalk to his car. He's a teenager and *really* cute; even Marianne would think so. He's in brown cords and a white T-shirt with the sleeves rolled up. The car behind him honks and he waves it by. He's got nice white teeth and smells of good cologne. "I thought there was a store nearby?"

I like how he looks, brown eyes and dark hair in a short do. I'm starting to get a little tingle. I point to the right. "Yeah, 7-Eleven. Three blocks, at the corner of Wesley."

"Well, I'm dense," he laughs, "because I can't find it. I've gone by there twenty times."

He smiles and I blush. I tip my head down and look up at him. I shrug.

"You think maybe you'd show me?" he asks, reaching over to open the passenger door. *Click.*

Tingles for sure now, but I shake my head no. "I have to stay here."

"Oh, okay. I understand," he says, but doesn't shut the door. "Thanks anyway." He looks sad. "You're very nice."

On an impulse, I get in the car.

"Go straight," I say, pointing. I can feel my cheeks get warm. What the hell am I doing? What if my mother comes home, or one of our nosy neighbors sees me and tells? I don't even know this boy. Why am I not scared?

At 7-Eleven, we pull into a back space, away from other cars. He is soooo cute! Without saying a word, he helps me into the back. He's got a twin mattress there and three huge red and black pillows, like something out of a '60s movie. He kisses me. We fool around and when I stop him, it's fine. He understands, leans back, smiles. It's very romantic. His breath smells faintly of menthol and cigarettes.

He kisses me again and this time, we go further.

After, he lights a cigarette and offers me one. I take it but I don't inhale; the smoke makes me cough.

"You're really beautiful," he says and I smile. "How old are you?"

"Almost fifteen." I lie. I'll be thirteen in August.

"Can I see you again?"

"I don't know."

"Just in case, here's my phone number," he scribbles on the back of an envelope. "If you call, I'll pick you up. Anywhere you say." We kiss and he cups my face in his hand, just like Jonathan did. "I love your green eyes."

I smile as I walk home after. I wish I could tell Davy about him, or at least Marianne. "His name is Charles," I'd say. "He just turned seventeen. Very handsome. He wants me to call him. You'd like him. He thinks I'm beautiful."

I get home just in time to climb into my bed before Mom and them get back. I really am flushed now and don't have to pretend at all.

I see Charles three more times. I tell Mom I'm working with a teacher after school, then meet him out back behind the field. We drive somewhere we can park without getting hassled. We don't talk a lot, but it's okay. He's sweet. He makes me feel important.

Usually, when he drops me back off, I scramble out of the van, but this time, I sneak one last kiss. My luck — it's just as Hugo Leone and Fat Ralph are coming out of soccer practice. Charles drives off, but I can tell by their faces that they saw everything.

"Sicko!" Hugo growls, him and Fat Ralph coming up close behind me as I hurry toward the street to get home. They can't do anything — the coach and rest of the team are around — but still they surround me, keep me from moving.

"Who should we tell first?" Ralph says. "Marianne?"

"Hell, no, we got to tell Sister Mary Margaret. Or maybe Mother Superior."

"Leave me alone," I mutter.

"That's a sin against God, you know," Hugo says, and they both laugh. "You'll be expelled."

"Maybe even tomorrow," Ralph says, and they high-five each other, then abruptly turn the other way.

I never call Charles again. I'm scared to. I watch Sister Mary Margaret. Nothing. Marianne doesn't seem any different, either. Only me. Now I try get to school just as class starts and leave immediately after. Still, it feels like they're always watching.

*     *     *

It's late summer when I have my revelation. I'm finally thirteen. Mom makes me a birthday cake and fixes pot roast and potatoes for dinner, my favorite. She gives me a pullover sweater the exact same green as my eyes. And hers. I try it on. She smiles and leans in to give me a little kiss on my cheek.

"Makes up for last year, huh?" she whispers.

Last year Elvis Presley died — on my birthday. When Mom heard, she dropped my cake, then locked herself in her room and didn't come out for three days. Nobody knew what to do, not even Dad.

All of this rambles around my head as Davy and I ride BART home from class. I'm wearing my new sweater. It's still light out even though we have late classes in summer. I think about last year, how weird it was that no one but Marianne told me Happy Birthday. Everybody worried about Mom instead. I can't remember what I thought, if I put it together about Elvis. We never talked about it.

We never talked about Dad or the divorce, either. Or Paul. Or Grandma, for that matter — or even Uncle Bobby. This makes my stomach hurt. Which makes me take a deep breath. Which brings me to a brand-new thought.

I know what's wrong with our family.

I sit straight up, blink my eyes.

It's so simple.

It's the secrets. They weigh us down. They keep us from knowing things clearly; they cover our lives like those shrouds on the mummies in the museum. We can't hold them all, so we pretend they aren't there. Except that makes everything worse, like when my finger got infected and the doctor had to lance it open, so the pus could all come out. It had nowhere else to go.

Across the aisle, Davy nods his head and twitches his feet, lost in his music. What's *his* secret? Is he sleeping with Isabelle? How about Marianne? She knows the most about our family. What does she not tell? What happened with Dad and Paul? I know Kaitlyn has secrets, she must, she never talks to anybody anymore. Sometimes I catch her standing in the living room, staring at the statue of Mother Mary.

Secrets can make you crazy. Look at Grandma.

I can't believe I didn't think of this before.

It will change everything. I don't have to be the kid in the corner, the one who doesn't fit in. I can be the one who makes everything better.

"What's wrong with you?" Davy asks, as the train pulls in and we stand and wait to file off.

"Nothing."

"Then why are you smiling?"

"You'll find out," I say.

He shakes his head at me. "Weirdo."

## {2}

The family meeting's called a week from Friday; I can think of nothing else. I know Mom won't give me another chance. She surprised me by agreeing in the first place.

"But why your father and Paul?" she said, when I asked her. We were in the living room, standing near Jesus.

"Because I have something I need to tell everyone. It's really, really important."

"All right then." She gives me a look like she knows what I'm going to say, and I feel like smiling. "I'll do what I can."

Still, I'm kinda scared. Each day, I consider the words. They've got to be perfect, exactly right, so we can be a family again. So the secrets will stop. I'm thinking on this so hard after school on Tuesday, I don't see Hugo Leone and Fat Ralph Conifer until I practically bump into them. They stand there grinning like a couple of cartoon hyenas.

"*What?*" I say with such force, it surprises me as much as it does them. For a second they don't talk.

"You know what," says Fat Ralph.

"Time to put the trash in the garbage can . . ." they sing-song together, with those stupid expressions.

"Oh, fucking grow up, would you?"

Ralph's mouth drops open, which makes me laugh. They step away;

I take this as a sign. The family meeting is right. Things do change, standing up for myself is necessary. This is the proof I need. I smile all the way home.

Friday morning finally arrives. School goes on forever and dinner's baked chicken, but I can't make myself eat a thing. Mom says nothing. After, we pray as usual. Still, nothing. Did she forget? Change her mind?

Then the doorbell rings and like magic, my father's here. Nobody knows what to say. He comes in, nods at Mom, tries to smile. He checks out the shrine. I remember that he's never been here before; I wonder if Jesus makes him uncomfortable too. I smile. He winks back. Then Paul knocks. He doesn't smile. He sees Dad and starts to back out. Marianne goes to him and the two talk, quietly. More silence. Paul sees Jesus and rolls his eyes.

"Shall we start?" Mom asks, and I nod.

"Start what?" Davy asks. "What's going on?"

"Would you all please sit on the sofa?" I say.

"What are they doing here?" Davy continues.

"Be still and sit down," Mom answers, looking at me. "We're having a family meeting."

"About time," Paul mutters. His voice is deeper than I remember. His eyes shift back and forth; he stays far away from Dad.

Mom sits in the center. I stand by the shrine. My family settles. I'm conscious of Jesus to one side, Mother Mary to the other. I suddenly feel very young. What am I doing? Who do I think I am? I push the questions away. This is right. It needs to be done. A second later, I begin. I'm not even nervous.

"I have something important I want to say."

My voice rings out clear and almost loud. Davy rolls his eyes. Mom sits straight up, motionless. I take my dramatic pause, exactly like I practiced. They lean into it, just slightly, into me, waiting. I hear the traffic, the clock ticking, Kaitlyn breathing raspily through her mouth.

"For Christ's sake," blurts my dad, "get on with it!"

Mom shoots him a look.

"Oh, for Christ's sake," he says again, but sits back. Paul sighs. I don't let it ruin the moment; I start again.

"I have something important I want to say. I couldn't say it before, but now I can. I don't have to keep it secret anymore." I smile.

Mom smiles back.

"Shit, Jason, don't —" Marianne says.

"I'm gay."

When you flip on a lightbulb and then turn it off again, the image hangs there, in front of your eyes, like the smiles on the faces of my family do now. That's okay. I know what's coming. I grin even harder. Any second, they'll be up and hugging me, jumping around and happy, like Davy getting Fritz. My mother will have one less thing to worry about. One less family secret.

That image fades. All eyes turn blurry, like when Grandma's old dog died; the light in them disappears, pulled back.

I still smile. I can't seem to stop.

In the room, absolute stillness, except the pounding of my heart. Finally, my dad stands and my heart slows a bit — he'll fix it. He can fix anything. He's my dad. He has a chair set up in the garage, just for me.

"Well, son," his voice is low. He blows air out of pursed lips. He doesn't look at me. "I guess it's between you and your mother now."

"Dad?" My voice is tiny.

He won't turn. He doesn't say good-bye. He won't look at me, Mom, Paul, anyone. He lifts his coat from the rack, opens the front door, and disappears.

"That was stupid," Paul says to me, close up by my face so only I hear. "Really stupid." Marianne takes his arm and they head for the front door too. Davy's mouth hangs open. Kaitlyn looks at Jesus, crosses herself. My mother's a statue. I become one too. The door closes behind Paul; Marianne looks back into the room. Finally, Mom speaks.

"Go to your rooms. Pray for your brother."

"Look, Mom —" Marianne starts.

"NOW."

They leave without another sound. Marianne catches my eyes and sends a kiss with her lips. It almost looks like she's crying.

"Close your doors," Mom orders. Suddenly, it's me and her and Jesus. She picks up her rosary and turns the beads over and over in her hands, staring at them a good long moment before speaking. My eye itches but I don't dare scratch it.

"Where did you hear that word?" Her voice is monotone, low, under normal.

"In San Francisco."

"From who?" Each syllable is pronounced, sharp, a weapon. Like her eyes slicing up and through me.

"Lots of people."

"What does that mean — 'lots of people'? Which people?"

"Lots of people. Tons."

She pauses. I cannot look away as much as I would like to. I have to breathe faster to keep oxygen in my lungs.

"All of those people are going to hell." Ice.

"No, there's too many." I'm not talking back; I want to explain.

"They are going to hell, Jason. Do you understand?"

"Yes." But I don't.

"Do you want to go to hell?"

"No." Barely a whisper.

"Good. Take it back."

"I can't." It does not occur to me to lie, to agree, to pretend.

"You take it back or you will burn in hell." She growls her words.

"But, Mommy, if God made me gay, then — "

"Don't you dare say that word with His name!" She raises her arm. I think she'll hit me; instead, she crosses herself. Still, I inch back.

"But if God made all the people then he must have wanted me to be — this way. Why would he send me to hell?"

A pause. "This is the worst kind of sin, Jason."

"But —" I feel myself shrinking. Her eyes are not real to me, they're demon eyes. My skin turns cold. My legs shake.

"The *worst* kind."

"What can we do?" My voice comes from outside my body.

"You have to take it back."

I wait to see if I can, then shake my head no, barely.

"Take it back."

"I can't."

She blinks, then moves to the room I share with my brother. I hear Davy rush to his bed as she opens the door.

"No son of my mine is going to hell." Her voice is higher now. She snatches clothing from drawers and stuffs it into my backpack. She marches back to the front door and opens it. She tosses out the backpack and grabs my arm. "You can't live here." She shoves me onto the porch.

"But, please, I —"

"Call me when you change your mind."

She starts to close the door, but stops. "If you go to your father's, I'll have you both locked up." I still can't look away. "You know what the police do to boys like you, don't you?" Her face gets dark and old as she leans in close to me. "They hook you up to electrical wires and burn you till you stop. Is that what you want?"

I shake my head no.

She sighs. Pauses. Speaks. "Do you take it back?"

"I can't."

I imagine fire will shoot from her eyes and I will burn right there. But she just shakes her head and straightens up, composes her face, becomes beautiful again.

"Go on, then. See how you like living with perverts."

# 1978

## TWO YEARS BEFORE

## LOS ANGELES COUNTY

{1}

Mission Bay, near San Diego — one more white middle-class badge of success. It's what my dad lives for. We go for a month each summer and rent a house along the ocean. Not to *do* anything, just to show we can afford it. I can't believe I'm part of this family. I can't believe they don't know shit about anything.

"How about I'll stay here," I say, the week before we're scheduled to go. Already Chelsea won't be joining us; she has to work. Mom's doing dishes and I'm at the kitchen table, eating a tuna sandwich. She whirls around like I slapped her.

"Fine. Do what you want," she snaps, glaring. "What do I care?'"

"Hey, I want to go, but the band has gigs."

"I just told you — I don't care." She goes back to washing. "Your father's not going either. It'll be great. You can hang out with him. I'll spend my time with your grandma."

This changes everything. "Why isn't he going?"

"Why do you think, Doug?" Like it's my fault. "He has to work, of course." She wipes her hands on her apron, starts putting dishes away.

"Why do I try so hard?" she mutters as she drops plates on top of each other, that stupid smile plastered on her face. I used to love watching her work in the kitchen. She seemed so completely in charge of things. Now she's too skinny, her face looks wrinkled and old. Now I feel sorry for her.

But I'm definitely not staying home alone with my dad.

First day, I meet up with the same guys I always see there and we hike over to where the out-of-staters park their RVs. They always leave their kids' bikes lying around. *Always.* Every year. We each snatch one and pedal like hell. We splash some paint on 'em, change the decals, and voilà! New bikes. I take the Sting Ray; riding at that angle, my hip barely hurts.

Now, a week into it, we're lounging on the cliff, trying Quaaludes for the first time. This kid Chris got a bottle from his sister.

"Dude, I can't feel my lips," I say, smacking them together. Not much else either. It's nice, easy. "What happens if you take two?"

"Check it out." Chris shakes out another pill.

I swallow it and ease myself down onto the ground, shading my eyes with both hands so I can take in the bluffs from this point of view. The sky sure is blue. This is a good high—relaxing and mellow, makes me feel like I could do anything. Conquer the world. Slap my dad upside the head and tell him what a loser he is.

Or even—I smile—do Dead Man's Drop.

I grab my bike and race toward the housing development that ran out of money. There's a street up there that just *ends.* No barrier, nothing. It's been talking to me for a while, but now—now's the time.

"Let's ride!" I yell and speed off. The guys scramble for their bikes.

From the top, tipping the front of my bike over the edge, the incline looks steeper than I remembered. The street on this side of the hill goes almost straight down and levels out just before it stops. A person could get seriously hurt. Do I care? Not much. Because, you know what? You only live once.

I push off. Wind whips my hair back and makes me yell "Yeeee haaaaaa!" like I'm some old-time ride-'em cowboy. I whoosh past the guys; they're a blur, yelling and egging me on. At the end of the street, the asphalt curls up just a bit and I'm launched up into the sky— flying! I'm Superman!

Then I'm in the Bay.

My bike's totaled, but hey, I stole it, didn't I? I manage to avoid my hip. My arm gets scraped on a rock, but it's worth it. And I'm still high. We head over to Chris's. Smoke some pot. He's met a couple girls and they come over but I'm still not good around chicks, so I let the guys tell my story. I don't get back to my place until late.

No lights on, and Mom's car is gone. Front door's not locked. Grandma's passed out on the couch. I scarf leftovers from dinner and settle on the couch just as the phone rings.

"Dad's been sleeping with his secretary," Chelsea says, not bothering with hello. "I don't know how Mom found out but she did. She drove all the way up, and Doug, she tried to shoot the bitch."

"Wait, what?" This is not making sense. "Chels—are you high?"

"No! I swear. She got Dad's gun from the house and went to his office."

"Did she actually—"

"No, but she scared the hell outta her. Dad called the cops."

"Is she in jail?" I almost hope she is. That'd be the end of him.

"No, he changed his mind when they got there. They're both home now. Where have you been? I've been calling you all night."

"Out. Damn. What a bastard."

"I know. She shoulda just shot *him*."

\*　　　\*　　　\*

I spend the last two weeks alone with Grandma. My father insists, since he already paid for it. I talk to Chels almost every day and we both agree that now, finally, our parents will get a divorce.

"I could stand that," I tell Chelsea.

"Hell, yeah. I might even move home," she agrees.

I stay high most of the time, mellow highs, nothing hardcore. I write a shitload of music. Finally, Chelsea comes to pick me and Grandma up. She's got bad news.

"No divorce," she announces. "They're going to counseling."

"As they should," says Grandma, from the backseat. Neither one of us listen; she's my dad's mom. We drop her off and head toward the house. Chelsea keeps the car running.

"I don't want to see him," she says.

"Me either." I get out. "I'll call you if anything good happens."

Dad's coming out of the kitchen as I open the front door. He's holding a Coors and a bag of chips. The first thing I notice is that I'm taller than he is—with my boots on, by at least an inch. We stand there, staring at each other like we're at the OK Corral, neither one sure who's going to draw first. I shut the door and he settles into his chair.

"Heard you went in the Bay," he says, not even looking at me, with this slimy smirk on his face.

"Heard you did your secretary."

The second it's out, I can't quite catch my breath. A nasty taste swims up in my mouth and my legs tremble. But I stand my ground. I stare right at him. I clench my fists so he can't see my hands shaking. What sounds like a jet plane starts to takes off in my head. But he doesn't swell. He doesn't even twitch. Color comes into his cheeks. He opens his mouth to speak, then closes it again. He walks the few steps to his chair and sits down. I still don't move. He guzzles the beer and opens the bag, then picks up his newspaper and ignores me.

## {2}

Craig's mom, Anne, waves to me as I come in the front door. They're having an end-of-summer party and our band is gonna play. Craig's cousin Nell, on the couch with a bunch of her friends, nods at me, lifts her hand. My mom doesn't like that I'm here. She disapproves of Craig too. I don't care. Craig and his mom are like family to me.

Craig calls from the patio and I go out and pick up a beer. He's blasting Wasted Youth now; our band's set up to play later in the backyard.

*"Raised by money they been deprived*
*Look at them with bleeding eyes . . ."*

When we play our set, I trash my voice but everybody loves us. I lose track of the beers, greyhounds, peppermint schnapps, and screwdrivers I'm drinking. The last thing I remember is being shirtless on Craig's bed with a girl whose name I think is Peggy, wondering if I'll finally get laid.

Then it's morning, and I'm on the couch, sunlight drilling into my brain, drool crusting around my mouth. I drank way too much, I've got that sick-drunk feeling and I need to throw up or maybe just run my head into a wall. I put my hands up to rub it.

*"What the—?!"*

Somebody cut my hair! I don't know who; I could have done it myself, for all I remember. It's short, really short. I drag myself to the bathroom, stepping over bodies still passed out on the floor, and check it out in the mirror. It's barely an inch long, with a tag in the back made of the old long hair. Someone braided that. Peggy?

"Oh, man," Craig busts up when he sees me. "Your momma's gonna kick your ass."

"Who cares," I say, trying to play it off. It's not my mom I'm worried about. I seriously doubt my dad's gonna let this one go. "Hey. We still going surfing?"

Anne drops us off. People stare. Older people move away, put a hand on their kids. I like this. Walking on the beach with my new hair makes me feel older somehow. We paddle out to where the surf Punks are, to wait for a wave.

"Check it out—fresh cuts!" announces one of the surf Punks; his buddies bust out laughing.

"Check out the fag tag!" yells another.

"You got a fag tag, man," still another Punk calls to me. "Are you a fuckin' fag, man?"

I hold up my finger, pretend I don't care, but the second I'm back at Craig's house, I chop it off. "I'm gonna do a Mohawk," I say.

"No, man, you got to grow that from scratch or it don't count." He grins. "But I got an idea." He gets his cousin to bleach it bright orange.

My parents are eating dinner when I come in. My father's mouth freezes before he can yell at me for being late. My mother's hands fly to her cheeks.

"Oh my God, Douglas, what did you do?!"

"Like it?" I ask.

"No. I do not. I do not like it at all."

"Oh well, sorry, too late now, huh?" I sit, ready to bolt if my dad comes after me. I'm not about to be Carl.

"What are your teachers going to say?" Mom gets up and comes over to look at it closer. She almost but not quite touches it. My dad keeps shoving food into his mouth. Suddenly, I *want* him to say something. I want "stupid asshole" to come spewing out. I want to see what I'll do. I don't get the chance. He just keeps slopping in the food.

*       *       *

My outside now matches what goes on in my head. I'm coming into my own. Finally. My hair's a badge announcing who I am. I get a new tattoo to celebrate—Evan does it, a death head, up on the back of my shoulder. Two days later, I shave all my hair off and start to grow my Mohawk for real.

Start clubbing—for real.

Meet PUNKS, lots of them, including the other Punk from my school.

"What's your name again?" I ask her.

"Rosie."

"Rosie at the Roxy," I tease. Her boyfriend comes up behind her.

"This is Mark," she says as he slips his arm over her shoulders. "Doug," she points to me.

"Hey," Mark says, his eyes darting. "Seen ya around." He's way older, maybe twenty-five. I like his tattoos.

"Doug's in my grade at school. People pick on him too."

"No shit," I say, thinking of just last week, when a bunch of jocks surrounded me, pushed me back and forth, called me names. The vice principal walked right past. Didn't do a thing.

"Yeah?" Mark says, checking me out more carefully now. "Guy your size, they shouldn't get away with a lot."

"They don't." At least they won't from now on.

"Maybe you could keep an eye on Rosie too, huh? Save me from having to come out there and kick some ass, probably get arrested."

Hell yeah, I'll watch out for Rosie.

We all have to take care of our tribe.

# 1978

## TWO YEARS BEFORE

### SAN FRANCISCO

{1}

The front door clicks shut. The deadbolt slides into place. The porch light goes out. I hold my breath. She's just punishing me. Like when we stand against the wall. I'll wait, very still, until she opens the door. We'll pray.

A car honks, then another.

An eighteen-wheeler grinds to a stop.

I blink. Is Davy watching from our window?

My mother's probably kneeling before Jesus. I feel the yard under my shoes. My backpack strap on one shoulder. A leaf dances its way from the tree next door, touching ground and then swirling once again. The breeze makes cold tracks down my face. I'm crying. I didn't even know it. I glance at my house, no lights on now at all. She's gone to bed.

I start to walk. I don't know what else to do.

My stomach growls; I wish I'd eaten that chicken. I slip my other arm through my backpack, feel in my pockets for the change from lunch. When is the last train? Midnight? One? I've only gone to the

BART station in the daytime, with Davy, when Mom drove and dropped us off. Will I find the way on foot? How long will it take? Should I run?

I decide I don't need to. I pass St. Andrews and realize I'll never have to see Fat Ralph Conifer or Hugo Leone ever again. I won't have to wear stupid robes and carry a heavy gold candle, or notice Sister Mary Margaret staring at me when she thinks I'm not looking.

So maybe it's okay, what's happened.

Maybe it's meant to be, maybe it's all going to be fine. I'll go to Castro Street and won't be afraid to talk because I'll live there too. I'll hold hands with boys right out in front of everyone. I'll smile and laugh and feel grand.

Night has transformed the train station. No cars in the parking lot, no people on the platform, only the bright overhead globes shining down in round splotches of light on the pavement. It's like some huge science fiction city. I smile. I'm having an adventure.

I don't see cops or security guys, but try out a story, just in case: *My grandparents had an emergency and had to drop me off, but you don't have to worry, both my parents are waiting at the station in San Francisco.* I like the idea of my parents waiting, except no one asks. The one old guy sweeping up glances over once, but that's it. I use the last token Mom gave me for going to Conservatory.

The train arrives and I get in a car. I'm all by myself. I sit on one side for a bit, then bounce over to the other. I go from car to car. I walk on the seats. I examine the lines on the map that say all the places that BART can take you. I wonder if I'm scared. I do dances like Davy, twitching my feet in combinations and playing music inside my head as the train zooms under the Bay.

I get off at the Civic Center station and head up toward Market Street. I plan to take exactly the same route I did when I discovered Castro the first time, except now, oh my God, Market Street is empty,

quiet — no trolleys, no cars, no people, only a scruffy black dog behind a garbage can, wolfing down dinner. He glances over, stares hard
a minute and growls, in case I was thinking of stealing it.

The bricks on the street sparkle with dew, like some secret army
of cleaners came in the night to polish away footprints. The light posts
gleam shiny black, their lamps like little suns glowing in the night.
And me? I'm the bravest boy ever, a knight on a quest, the killer of
dragons and the banisher of evil. I march alone down the center of
the biggest street in all of San Francisco! I shut my eyes for a few
steps, head back, arms out. Electricity hums from the streetcar wires
above me. When I stand still, I can feel the vibration of the cables running underneath.

I make a vow — I will always look forward now, never back. I will go
and live in my magical village and be myself and everything will be
happily ever after.

I expect this same stillness on Castro, but people seem to be coming out of everywhere. They're in the street, on the sidewalk. Voices
talk and laugh, people hug and kiss. Two guys have a lovers' argument and I put my hand to my mouth to keep from saying "oh!"
because I never knew gay people argued like everybody else. My
smile's bursting, my heart's happy. I tuck my bag under a bench near
a bar called The Phoenix and settle in to soak it all up. I especially love
the laughter.

"Hello, everybody," I whisper. "I'm back. I'm home!"

The grand enchantment doesn't last; cars drive off, people turn
corners, doors close, and business lights go dark. The street empties
and I figure it out — I got here when the bars were closing and now everyone's going home. Soon, the only person I see is behind the counter in the 24-hour donut shop. I can't go there, he'll call my mother or
the police.

I take a huge breath. The air's turned frosty. Wisps of the fog that sits above Twin Peaks drift past like wandering ghosts. I shiver and dig into my backpack to see what I have. My birthday sweater's right on top; I slip it over my head. I see my mom's smile when she gave it to me and I'm small again. I see her eyes, as she shut the door. Too many thoughts hit at once. I don't want them. I grab my backpack and walk.

Look forward, not back.

I go past the bar called Bears and the Castro Street Theater. They're showing *Whatever Happened to Baby Jane* and I stop to look at the poster of the scary-looking doll with her head smashed in. *"Sister, sister, oh so fair, why is there blood all over your hair?"* Creeps run down my back, then I remember this is where I first smelled Paco Rabanne, the cologne I love. I sniff — nothing now, but still, I get that little tingle.

I'm going to be just fine. I will. I'm sure of it. People are sleeping now — when they wake up, the magic will return. I'm here and nothing can hurt me. No more secrets.

I walk to the end of the block. I like the fog swirling in, getting thicker. I like the streetlamps making bright little circles on the sidewalk, tiny lit-up stages. I tiptoe around the edge of one, humming "The Dance of the Flirt," the solo Davy always got, the one I always wanted. I dance his steps (I didn't know I knew them!) and finish with a perfect double pirouette. I land exactly placed in fourth position, arms up and out, head thrown back, waiting for my applause. I laugh with the glory of it.

Light shines into a space between two buildings, pointing out a narrow alley. No garbage, not even paper or trash. A nook. A nook where I might just fit.

I brush back the dirt and lie down on my side to try it out. I cross my arms. I scoot my back against one wall, pull my knees up, and stick my backpack under my head. It's cozy. The walls of the buildings block the wind. The glow from the streetlamp is almost like the night-light plugged into the wall of my bedroom. More fog is swirling but I'm okay here, safe. It doesn't feel much different than being on the top bunk and staring at the ceiling, except here, the bed and the ceiling are sideways. I'll be fine.

With a long, slow sigh, I close my eyes.

A few minutes later, they fly open on their own. What have I done? My heart pounds, my body trembles. I have to go home. Everyone will be worried. I can't be out here all alone. I sit, pushing myself hard against the wall, clutching my backpack inside my knees. A wall of fog closes off the nook, wisps like hands reach in, tiny yellow spaceships float just feet away. I can't see buildings, just gray and then darkness. Every scary monster I ever imagined waits out there. My muscles lock. I can't find air. No one is coming to help.

There's a pause, like the world takes a breath, and from down deep inside me, I yell, right out loud, "Come on then!" I drop my backpack and stand straight up, lift both hands out to the gray and yell out again, "You want me? Come get me!"

Nothing.

It's just a street. It's only fog.

## {2}

What the hell's going on?

A flash, I remember — my family, all together, eyes fading, last night's fog. I'm in The Castro. I'm in my village. My stomach gurgles as I sit up. My right arm has pins and needles. I rub it and peer out — not too many people, but at least the street's alive again. I stand and stretch, slip around the corner, lean on my building. I cross one leg over the other like I'm waiting for a bus, like I'm supposed to be here.

"Oh my! Hello."

The voice startles me. I realize the wall to my right is a restaurant, with tables set up outside. Two guys are having coffee and croissants. They smell delicious, the guys do — clean and crisp. They're both smiling. I smile back.

"Visiting friends?" Dark-haired guy glances at his buddy in that grown-up-knowing kind of way. I shake my head again and take a chance, point to my nook.

"You slept there?" Blond man asks, his smile fading. "Are you all right?"

I nod. "I lost my bus money."

They chuckle a little. "Oh, honey, we all know that one," dark-haired guy says, putting his hand on blond man's arm. "Not to worry." He hands me a ten dollar bill. "Get breakfast, then call home, all right? Promise? Your mom's probably worried sick."

"Thank you." I smile.

"Ah! Look at those eyes," dark-haired guy says, touching my arm lightly. "You have beautiful eyes."

I blush. He winks.

*　　*　　*

*"You have beautiful eyes."*

I stroll down Castro, backpack in place and ten bucks in my pocket. I get a seat by the window at the Twin Peaks, order a chocolate croissant and a cup of coffee. I feel very grown-up, sitting here on my own. I wonder what people are thinking? That I'm older than I actually am? That I'm waiting for my lover? I sip the coffee and make a face. It's not at all like it smells — it's bitter! I use all the packets of sugar and most of the cream, then sip and smile. People stroll past. Two guys jog by in shorts and tank tops. Across the street, a man is sketching another man at the table in front of a café.

I hear my mother's voice: *"It is the very worst sin, Jason."*

How can that be true?

She doesn't understand. She thinks it's like Uncle Bobby.

Suddenly, I know something. Marianne was telling the truth. My Uncle Bobby did take pictures of me. One time. That's all. I was six. At the old house, up in the attic that my dad turned into a bedroom for us three boys. Uncle Bobby didn't live there; he stayed at Grandma's. But babysat us, a lot. Maybe that's why I was alone with him. I remember him calling me over to show me pictures of Paul.

"This is what big boys do. See how much fun Paul's having? Would you like to have some fun too?"

It felt creepy and I didn't know what to say. He was my uncle, after all — and Paul didn't look unhappy in the picture. He just looked naked.

"I have to go downstairs," I mumbled.

"Okay. I guess you're not a big boy yet, are you?" Uncle Bobby said, in a sad voice. "I thought you were."

"I am too a big boy."

"I don't think so."

"Yes I am," I said and took off my clothes. He told me how to sit and then snapped the camera. It made that *sshhhhh-ka* Polaroid sound as the picture came out. He changed my position and did some more. He set it up so we could take a picture together, and started to take off his clothes. The back door creaked open, and Marianne yelled, "Anyone home?" Uncle Bobby zipped up his pants and got me into my clothes. His face made me think of creeping lizards.

"If you tell, Paul will get in bad trouble," he said, and now his voice was scary too. "They'll send him away and people will beat him up. He'll never ever come back."

What Uncle Bobby did — that was a sin. But that's not being gay. Being gay isn't about hurting people.

I glance up, can't help it — I expect to see Jesus above me in the sky, with those eyes, watching.

*"All those people are going to hell."*

I sigh and finish my last sip of coffee. The man who's being sketched takes a look at the picture and laughs, loud and bell-like. They hug. I smile along with them. If those are the people who are going to hell, and if heaven is for people like my mother — then it's simple. I know exactly where I want to be.

I try to picture what Mom's doing now. Did she sleep well? What will she tell Davy and the girls? Will they miss me? Will she tell my dad? Will he come looking for me or did he mean what he said? What will she say to the nuns when they call to see why I'm not in school?

"I'm so sorry, Sister," she'll say, "but Jason can't come to school anymore. He had to go to hell."

"It's about time!" Sister Mary Margaret will answer.

This makes me smile.

"Anything else?" the waitress asks, smiling too. Her eyes are deep brown. Did my mom ever look that young?

I shake my head no.

"Great eyes!" she says and winks as she takes my ten, brings me change. I leave a two-dollar tip and head out to my street.

The fog's resting on the top of the hills but the sky is very blue — one of those beautiful San Francisco days. I glance at a clock in a store. I'd be in Madame Nevonski's class right now — we'd probably be going across the floor. Did Davy ride on BART alone this morning or did Marianne have to go with him? She wouldn't want to, I know, but if Mom said —

*Stop.*

I shake my head and push these thoughts away. I have beautiful eyes, *great eyes,* and this whole day to myself. Time to move forward.

When the stores open, I go into All American Boy and try on stone-washed Levi 501s and a white shirt. I smile at myself in the mirror and at the clerk who finds my size. He's very cute. I use the rest of the ten for a Coke and two Snickers bars, then spend my usual Saturday, wandering. I tingle and I smile. I'm here — all of me together, just like with Jonathan Grant.

By seven, however, I'm starving and now, I have no money. What was I thinking, leaving that waitress two bucks? What do I do now? Can I use the same story? I check around to find someone who looks friendly, who might help — and spot clam chowder sitting all by itself on an outdoor table, in a round sourdough bread bowl. It's almost full. No one's paying attention, the people eating have obviously left — there's a tip.

Should I grab the soup? A trickle of sweat runs down my left side. I reach over the bushes, pause a second to consider the spoon, then snatch that too. Hey — why not? I'm already going to hell.

I sit on a bench down the street, eat my soup, and watch the sun go down. The sunset is grand. Life is grand. I'm here in my village on a Saturday night, Paco Rabanne and tingles galore. I can stay up till I get sleepy, then crawl into my little nook. Things are already turning out fine.

Something wakes me in the night. Loud talking, and flashing red and blue lights. Did she find me? Am I busted? I hug one wall and peek into the street. A cop and a taxi driver are arguing; the taxi driver has an accent like Madame Nevonksi's. A homeless guy sits on the curb nearby, cussing at something that's not really there, moaning, holding his head. The taxi driver insists to the cop that he didn't see the guy, didn't mean knock him over the hood of his taxi. He's mad because now it has a dent.

The faces of the people watching glow like my dad's velvet paintings, which makes them seem not quite real. They talk about the man who sits babbling, laughing at him, even though blood oozes from his nose and one side of his face got mangled on the pavement. The cop makes the people leave, and helps the homeless guy, still cussing, into the back of the patrol car.

It's hard to get back to sleep. I don't feel quite as safe. I have to make myself think good things only — the way The Castro looks in early morning, the guys who gave me money. The laughter of couples. The freedom of being where it's okay to be myself. My beautiful eyes.

## {3}

"You told me the same story three days ago, little man." The guy looked nice when I asked him, but not now. Now he's pissed. He snatches my arm and pulls me close, leans down so he's right in my face. "You want to hustle, do it on Polk. This is my street. I'll call the cops."

I yank away and run like hell. I hide in my nook for hours. I'm shaking; I can't seem to stop. How stupid could I be? I told the same exact story in the same exact place every day this week. What if he does call the cops? I know about the electrical wires they hook you up to. My mom said.

How am I going to eat? I don't dare ask anybody on Castro but I don't feel safe anywhere else. I feel like I stand out now — my clothes are filthy, my underwear stinks, both pairs, my hair's getting matted. I keep my eye out for food on tables, but my luck's disappeared. I go the next two days without eating. Food is all I think about. I get dizzy when I stand up too fast; my stomach feels like it has knives inside. Then I stop being hungry. This, I know, is a bad sign. Should I go home? I can't. Ask for help? I can't do that either.

For the first time, I notice how people dump perfectly good food into trash cans — unfinished sandwiches, half-empty cans of soda. I could snatch something pretty easily, except what if someone sees me and calls the cops? I slip into the alley behind All American Boy. No one's around so I check out the Dumpster. Busboys drop bags of stuff here all the time. I open the lid. The smell makes me gag, but at least I'm hidden. I climb up on a crate and peer down. A white plastic bag sits on top.

Holding my breath, I tear it open. Half a turkey sandwich appears in a goulash of other food; it's wrapped up in paper and there's only one bite taken. I bring it out with thumb and forefinger. The best I can, I brush off whatever's sticking to it and pick away the part that's bit into. I open my mouth, then close it. How can I eat someone else's garbage? Then my stomach cramps and I double over with pain.

It takes me several minutes to talk myself into the first bite, but only thirty seconds to polish the whole thing off and go back in for more. I remember the scruffy black dog I saw when I first got here. I'd growl now too. That was the best sandwich I've ever eaten.

\*       \*       \*

For almost a whole week now, not one word has come out of my mouth. It's like at school, except I never go home and nobody fixes my dinner.

"Good morning, Jason, how are you today?" I say out loud, to see if I still know how. "Just fine, thank you very much," I answer, making myself smile.

That evening, I follow a group of kids coming out of All American Boy. They're around a lot, always looking like they've got someplace to go. Always laughing too, having a good time. I see them up in Dolores Park, sometimes with a bunch of other kids. Tonight, I trail them as they go over to Polk Street. Now I'll see what that guy was talking about.

It's clearly a "gay street," but way different than Castro. There are kids on street corners. It's loud, lots of traffic. A couple of boys get into a fistfight a little ways down, calling each other all kinds of "whore" and "bitch." The other boys laugh at this too, then go their separate ways.

One of them climbs up on a bench. He can't be any older than me. I notice there are other boys on other benches all around the street, maybe two to a block, in front of stores and bars. I'm wondering how this all works when, all of a sudden, the boy I followed jumps down and slips into a nearby alley. The other kids disappear too, so I duck into a drugstore and pretend to be looking at combs. A cop car cruises down the street.

How did they know?

When I venture back out, the kid's already back and a silvery blue Pontiac has stopped in front of him. The driver leans over to talk. The hand he puts on the passenger door is fat and fleshy and pale; I can see his face only in silhouette. The boy climbs in the car. I follow them around the corner. The car parks and the boy's head disappears. I'm not stupid; I know what he's doing. That's his business; I don't really care. I wait anyway. I'm not sure why, maybe to see how he looks when he comes out.

*     *     *

I can't get the nerve to tell my bus money story again. I doubt if it would work now, anyway. I look different — not fresh like when I got here three weeks ago. But I've learned a few things — like, you can't keep underwear clean so it's best not to wear any. Like, people drop change everywhere and you can find a least a couple dollars a day, if you really look. Like, there's a sixth sense you get about how to take care of yourself. That laundry is cheapest down at Angel's on Mission. Easy too, you put in everything but your pants, and pay attention. People mostly don't use all their dry time — you can usually get minutes for free, if you're quick.

I know it's best to not to go the same gas station all the time to wash up; attendants get nosy. Going to the same Dumpster is good — you can keep track of what's fresh. Oh, and the 24-hour donut shop gives out freebies to street kids if you come in after eleven o'clock. The guy who runs it is named Tony and he never calls the cops. Lots of kids hang out there. Mostly, they're friendly.

My nook's still good. I find a green striped blanket somebody tossed out and an old blue and white comforter that I sleep on. I stay way to the back and sometimes tuck my backpack into the very farthest corner, so I won't have to carry it all day. I make sure not to let anyone see me slip in. Castro isn't quite as grand as I once thought, but it's okay. I'm not sorry I'm here. I love the city, especially Union Square. I sit there for hours and watch people.

I miss my dad, and Marianne. Sometimes Davy too. I know he thinks of me, misses me, wonders what I'm doing.

I see the kid from Polk Street a lot now. He's got a buddy who's older, like maybe seventeen, and another one around our age. I don't think they sleep here. The older guy kind of reminds me of Paul. I like his face; it's wise, like he knows a lot of stuff. Tonight he's strolling by himself. It's around two in the morning. I'm usually not out, but I couldn't sleep. I expect he'll walk on past, like usual, but he stops.

"Why you always watching me?" he asks.

"I'm not."

"Yeah, you are. What's your name?"

I almost lie. "Jason."

"Just got here?"

"No."

"Yeah you did."

I start inching back.

"Don't freak, Jason, I won't hurt you. I'm Tommy." He holds out his hand. "Pleased to meetcha."

I take the hand he holds out to me, but don't know what to say.

"Want some coffee?" he asks. I follow him to the donut shop. We slide in a booth with two other boys.

"Nick. Adam. Jason," Tommy says, pointing at each of us. "Two coffees, Tony? And a jelly roll if you have it."

Nick's telling Adam about a date he had with a fat guy. They don't pay much attention to me, but I sure do like the company, and the stories of what they do on the street.

"You work?" Adam asks, out of the blue. I blush, everybody's staring at me.

"No."

"Why not?" Adam wants to know. "You think you're too good? You think you're better than us?"

I shrug and mumble "no."

"Leave him alone, Adam," Tommy says.

"He's staring," Adam says. He reminds me of Davy.

Nick laughs. "You're so paranoid."

"Stop staring," Adam says, pouting.

Knowing people helps. I start hanging out at the donut shop every once in awhile. I hear how Tommy's from L.A. and got here three years ago. I learn stuff about surviving — about how you can stay under benches in Golden Gate Park when it rains. The avenue side. Or if you have change, you get on the green bus. You mind your business and curl up in the corner in the very back. If nobody complains, they usually let you ride all night. Sometimes I go for days without thinking about my family.

## {4}

"Waiting for someone?"

I'm startled. I've just snatched a piece of pizza left on a plate in front of the café. I stop, mid-bite. I didn't see the guy coming. "Excuse me?"

"I wonder if I might treat you to dinner? If you're not otherwise occupied."

"Sorry. I'm not a working boy."

He smiles, glances at the pizza in my hand. "I thought perhaps you were hungry."

His name is Nigel. We walk to a Chinese restaurant down the street. Inside is painted red and gold, with a huge dragon that takes up one whole wall. Its eyes follow me. I think of Jesus. Nigel gets a booth at the back. He orders tons of stuff I don't recognize and then tries to show me how to do chopsticks. I almost get it, but then drop my moo goo whatever on the tablecloth. He laughs and gets me a fork. I try everything he orders.

"Dessert at my place?" Nigel says just after the waiter sets down the fortune cookies. "I'm just around the corner."

I've heard all about sugar daddies from Nick and Adam. How they're usually older. How they give you a place to sleep and take good care of you, and all you have to do is be nice. Is this it? Have I met mine?

Nigel lives in a light blue apartment building just off Castro, a converted Victorian I've walked past a billion times. He unlocks the iron gate and we go through a tiny garden of miniature trees, with a small statue of a boy peeing into a pond. I giggle and Nigel smiles. He leads me up a spiral staircase and into his apartment. It's like nothing I've seen before. It's perfect. The colors, the shape of the furniture, the stuff hanging on the walls — all of it fits.

"Do make yourself at home," Nigel says. "I'll be out in a jiffy." I hear him turn on the shower.

I sit on the sofa, bounce on the cushy loveseat. Two tall bar stools whirl all the way around, I spin a couple of times on each of them. I can't stop smiling. I wander into the kitchen, which is arranged exactly how I would want mine, if I had one. I peek into the bedroom — the bed looks fluffy and has tons of pillows.

Nigel comes out in a pair of lounge pants and a dressing jacket. His hair's wet, combed back, and he smells delicious. He looks younger. He asks if I'd like to smoke some weed, which seems so weird I start to giggle again. He smiles.

"Haven't you ever been high?"

"Yeah, sure, lots of times, with my brother," I say, thinking of Paul, and how Davy and I sneaked it with him sometimes at the old house. "It just seems strange that you do it."

"How old are you, Jason?" he asks, as he brings out a water pipe that looks like it came from Ali Baba and his forty thieves.

"Almost seventeen," I lie, and shrug. "Just small."

After we smoke and nibble some amazing chocolate truffle cookies, Nigel runs me a bath with bubbles. The bathroom's all silver and white. He sits on a stool beside me and we talk as I wash up. Or he talks, mostly about his friend Jean Louis who's gone back to France to visit his mother. How much he misses him. How lonely he gets when he's gone. He washes my back. We have another dessert — green tea ice cream and some dark chocolate thing that melts in my mouth. Then we crawl in his supersoft king-size bed.

I wake before he does and wonder exactly how he'll ask me. "Jason, I simply must have you stay!" or "Dear boy, would you consider living here?" I run through the choices, smiling the whole time. I'll do it. I will.

I like him. I like the apartment, it feels safe. When he goes to work, I'll stay in and tidy up, maybe learn how to cook. He won't miss Jean Louis so much. Maybe he won't miss him at all. Maybe Jean Louis will have to find another place to live.

The alarm goes off. He opens his eyes.

"Hello," I say, smiling. I'm sitting cross-legged down at the end of the bed. It takes him a minute to speak.

"Jason," he says, obviously surprised that I'm here. "Good morning." He sits up and sighs, pats my arm. "I'm sorry, sweetie, I'm afraid I have to go to work."

"That's okay. I don't mind." I can feel how my face sparkles. He seems not to know what to say. He slides out of bed and puts on his robe. He leans to give me a kiss on the cheek.

"Darling boy, that means *you* have to go."

"Oh. Right. Sure. Okay." I slide off the bed, look around for my clothes. "Of course. Well, thanks for dinner, and everything."

"You're very welcome."

Out in the living room, I hear him turn on the shower running in the bathroom. I stop by the closed door.

"Nigel?" I call. "Do you think maybe I could borrow five dollars?" Where am I getting the guts to do this? "For the train home?"

"Of course, sweetie," he calls back. "My wallet's on the table, take the ten."

I take the twenty and slip out the door.

## {5}

All I notice this morning are people *together*: brothers and sisters, friends, moms and kids, lovers, husbands and wives.

And me. Alone.

My nook's not cozy now, it's grungy and cold. Kids in the park look sad and tired. Polk Street's filthy, with awful men, cheap bars. I don't know what to do with myself. I can't stay in The Castro today. I get coffee from Tony, then see Tommy and Nick coming. I head the other way. I end up where I always do when I'm feeling bad — down at Union Square. I climb up on a planter to watch the people.

I wonder what Davy's doing, if Dad's working on a new painting, what Marianne's having for lunch. An ache as big as the city wraps itself around my heart. This is no big adventure, I'm not a brave boy, I have no quest. I'm just another lonely street kid. Nothing special.

A woman with a little girl stares from the other side of the square. She's wearing yellow, my mom's color, except she's blond, like her daughter. Like me. She smiles as she sweeps a strand of her daughter's hair back from her face, then crosses toward me.

"Sweetheart, are you all right?" she asks. The little girl peers up, her head tipping back. Her hair shines in the sun, like a halo.

"Yes, ma'am."

"What's your name?"

"Tommy."

"When did you run away, Tommy?"

Is she a cop? A social worker? I should jump down now and run, but I don't.

"Is your family in the city?"

I shake my head no.

"East Bay?"

No again.

"Marin?"

I nod yes. I've never been there, but it sounds good.

"You have a mom?"

I nod. "She's at home."

"Okay. Tommy, you seem like a good boy and I want to tell you something really important. Mothers love their children more than life. Whatever happened, your mom will forgive you. I promise. She's probably worried sick."

She pushes a strand of hair out of my face. Her skin is smooth and cool. I think she's beautiful.

"Here's five dollars. Catch the Muni to Lombard then Golden Gate Transit across the bridge, all right? Check on the bus stop to see which number. Okay? Promise?"

"Yes, ma'am. Thank you."

"Who shall I say is calling?" the operator asks when I tell her I'd like to make this collect. I close the door to the phone booth to hear better. It took me a whole hour of thinking to decide that woman was right. How could my mom come find me? Or my dad? They don't know where I am. They've got to be worried sick.

"Her son."

"Which one?" Mom asks. Of course — Paul doesn't live there, either.

"Jason." I hold my breath, all of a sudden panicked, anticipating a click. Instead, she accepts the charges.

"Are you okay?" she asks, not sounding mad at all.

"I'm fine." My stomach relaxes. I smile. I'll be going home soon.

"Where are you calling from?"

"A friend's house."

The operator's stayed on the line.

"You are not, young man. You're at a pay phone in downtown San Francisco."

This silence is heavy. My stomach twists again. I hear Mom light a cigarette.

"Don't call me up just to lie to me, Jason." Her voice is flat now, like that night.

"I'm sorry, I didn't mean —"

"What do you want?"

"Can I come home now?" I blurt it out. I didn't know I was think-ing it.

"Are you done being gay?"

I sigh. "No."

She takes a drag of her cigarette and I hear the smoke whoosh out. I imagine her wearing her yellow dress, her hair up; I picture the smoke curling around the sides of her face.

"Look, Jason. You're my son and I love you. When you're done doing — whatever you're doing there — call me and you can come home."

"I can never be 'done,' Mom."

"Then you'll never come home, will you?"

*Click.*

*       *       *

Saturday, as I wash up and shampoo my hair in the Shell station sink, I feel a pang. If I were home, I'd have hot water and a shower and real shampoo. I'd be fooling around with Davy or getting ready for dinner or talking to Marianne. Mom would be finishing up setting the table and — I stop myself. I'm not home. I'm here and need to move forward. I finish up, duck out the door, and realize — so is Davy. Here. In the city. Right now. Not that far away.

I get to the Conservatory right when morning classes are ending. A woman I don't recognize stops me at the entrance gate.

"Yes?" she says, with a pleasant smile.

"Hi. I'm looking for my brother. Davy Commagere?"

"Oh." Her face darkens. "You're Jason, aren't you?" She checks the lock. "I'm sorry, dear, you can't come in."

"But . . ."

"Please go, or I'll have to call the police."

I back away. What did my mother tell them? The woman goes in and I sneak around the side and go in the main hall door. I see Isabelle. Her eyes widen; she pulls me around the pillar in the back corner.

"You're not supposed to be here," she whispers.

"I need to see Davy," I whisper back.

"I don't know, Jason."

"Please?"

"All right, okay. Stay here. I'll get him."

I squish as far into the corner as I can, wait until he rounds the corner with his sassy dancer's walk, towel draped over his shoulder, looking like always, except older.

"Hi," I say, stepping out, a big smile on my face. "You got taller."

He doesn't smile back. "You're not supposed to be here, Jason."

"That's what everybody keeps saying."

"You need to go." His voice sounds distant, cold.

"What?"

"Just go."

"But I want to talk to you."

"I can't be around you, okay?"

"Davy, I —"

"Go. Now. I mean it. Don't come back here."

"Look, whatever Mom said —"

"It's not Mom, Jason."

"I don't understand."

"I don't want to see you, okay?" He grabs Isabelle's hand and starts off.

"Davy!"

He whirls. "You're not my brother anymore. You got that? You're not my brother."

Neither one of them looks back. I should move, but I seem to have forgotten how. People slow down and stare, whisper. I hear my name. I think I see Michael. Down at the end of the hall, the woman from the gate starts walking toward me. A security guy is with her.

"He didn't mean that." I'm talking to myself, but I speak out loud. Somebody laughs.

"You! Jason!" the woman calls. I move then, out the hall door, around to the street.

"He didn't mean it." I say out loud, again. I hear the gate shut behind me. Boys and girls chattering. I keep walking. Davy's not used to me like this, he needs some time. It always takes him time. A few days, a week, a month, maybe, we'll be fine. I'll give him some time. He'll think about it, we'll get together and talk. This day will seem funny then. I look at my fingernails, oh boy, do they need cutting. I wonder if Nick still has that manicure set. Maybe we could also do a little trim on my hair.

This will all work out fine. Davy's my family. Families don't just stop.

# Late 1978

{1}

*"Fix me, fix my head! Fix me please, I don't wanna be dead!"*

Black Flag wails from the cassette deck and we all sing along. I could fly right now. Mark weaves between cars on the freeway and an asshole in a black pickup lays on his horn. Aw, rough life, poor baby had to brake. Four hands shoot out four windows, middle fingers pointing up.

"Fuuuuuck yoooooou!"

We chant it like a chorus, then laugh. I laugh loudest of all. I open my second beer and my brain spits out possibilities too vast to consider in one moment. This is what it's all about. Life. Life is good. The speed of this car. The music blasting. Rosie bouncing and singing next to me. Mark's brand-new scorpion tattoo curving around his neck.

In the backseat, Jack lights a joint. Jack's my age, my new hero; he dropped out of school. He stays with Mark sometimes. Mark's like my big brother now. He's twenty-five. I twist to get the joint and that shit-ass ice-pick pain shoots down from my bad hip all the way to my heel. It takes my breath. I hold the joint to my lips but can't inhale, not right away. I shift my weight; it doesn't help. How long is a metal pin supposed to hurt? Forever? Is that the price? Even now?

Who cares. It's only pain. Who cares.

I toke and pass the joint to Rosie, open a third beer. I chug the entire can, my miracle physical therapy. Mark stops at the light at the end of the off ramp.

"Montclair sucks, man," Rosie says, peering around at the low flat buildings and smoggy horizon.

"The world sucks, babe, get used to it," Mark tells her.

"Let's go to Irvine instead, okay? Social Distortion's playing free."

"Hell no. I'm getting that hundred dollars." Mark's beady eyes cut one way, then the other.

"Only if Doug wins the fight," Rosie argues.

"He'll win." Mark jabs my arm. "My boy can do anything."

He says it; I believe it. I never actually hit anyone, but shit. Like Mark says, I'm sure as hell big enough. If he thinks I can? You just watch.

Two Hells Angels rev their choppers in the lane to our right, all decked out in leather jackets with the sleeves cut off. One guy has a helmet that looks like a German soldier. *What's that supposed to mean, asshole? You think you're cool?* I like their death-head logo. I don't like their long stringy hair. I really don't like the fat-ass ugly redhead on the backseat of the first bike.

"Jeeeeezus H., what y'all sposed to be?" she asks with a twangy southern voice, smirking at us. "Is it Halloween already?"

"Fuck you," Rosie says back.

"Yes ma'am, she'll be glad to, come on out the car." The guy waggles his tongue between the V of two fingers. His girl laughs.

Like a shot, Mark's out of the driver's side. He stands on the floorboard and sends an empty whiskey bottle whirling over the Chevy. Roy chucks a second. They miss the bikers but glass shatters all over the street. Jack wraps his chain around his hand, I take hold of my blade, and we climb out too. Four Punks, three with buzz cuts and me with my four-inch purple Mohawk. All of us in boots, none of us smiling. One biker reaches for a club, the other for what looks like a short axe. The club guy faces us. The light turns green.

"Who the f—"

He doesn't get to finish that thought. A screech of brakes, car doors slamming—six more Punks closing in. Moving fast. We don't even know them; we don't even have to. Two women in the car behind Mark's slide down in their seats, mouths open, as the Punks from behind glide on past. We surround the Angels, two deep. Their eyes shift one way then the other, trying for a way out. Stupid assholes. They started the shit and now don't know what to do.

"Come on, Eddie," the redhead says, reaching for his arm. "It's not worth it, baby. Let's go."

Eddie tries to act cool getting on his bike. Like he's not scared shitless. Mark grabs his own crotch and pumps a couple times. We laugh. The guy flips us off but we just laugh harder. They have to drive through the broken whiskey bottles to get away. The light turns red. Sun glints off the rings Mark has through his lip. We high-five the cavalry and they pound the top of the car behind us walking back. The people in the line of cars just stare.

"Montclair sucks," Rosie mutters as we climb back in the car.

## {2}

Way too many people crowd in the basement of the Police Athletics League, all different kinds—Punks, hippies, jocks, *assholes*. The noise of them starts my head pounding. My hip still throbs but a healthy dose of Jack Daniels is taking care of that. The big problem now is, where's the music? Even a fight contest at a police hall ought to have music. I tip my flask. Jack snatches it away.

"You wanna get us arrested?"

"I don't fucking care." I grab it back, but pocket it. He's right—cops frame the room, each with a lame-ass grin on his face, the kind that never shows in the eyes. Like somebody told them this is how you look to make people like you. Like having a fight competition will make us get along and all that old hippie shit. I take a breath, wish I hadn't. The room stinks of B.O., pot, and bad breath. The ceiling's way too low. If there's an earthquake, we'll be squished, no chance of escape. Ceiling fans whir away but all they do is move the stink around. I have the urge to duck, run, get the hell out of here.

"Check it out," Mark says. He elbows his way forward. Rosie holds onto the back of his coat and takes me by the hand.

The boxing ring's dead ahead, set high, thick double ropes and everything. I half expect Rocky to come dancing down the aisle any second. The two guys in there now are big, one even taller than me. Both are older, like my brother's age, punching away. One's long-haired and greasy. The other wears a skintight P.A.L. T-shirt and sports a huge blond pompadour, plastered into place. He obviously wants us to know he's full-on rockabilly.

Suddenly this doesn't seem like such a good idea, a hundred dollars or not. If I knock the pin loose in my hip—or worse, snap off the top of it, I could be looking at a wheelchair for life. Whatever happens, it's going to hurt. I pull Rosie back toward me. She loses Mark's coat.

"What if I changed my mind?" I shout. They really should be playing music. "What if I want to go to Irvine right now?" Why am I talking to her? Why can't I just tell Mark no?

"Can't hear you!" she shouts back.

Mark's already at the ring, standing on an upside-down bucket to talk to the cop in the corner. He points and they glance my way at the very second Rockabilly's fist connects with Longhair's face. Longhair twirls, a snake of blood flying out of his nose as he plummets to the mat. Shit. He grunts as he hits, bounces, then stays still. The crowd goes crazy. Rockabilly holds both his arms up in victory, then turns to help Longhair stand. They grab gloves, smile like they're old buddies. The cop hands Longhair a black T-shirt, the same as the one Rockabilly has. When Longhair holds it up to show the crowd, he gets a round of applause. He grins like he's won a year's pass to Disneyland.

"Scared?" Mark asks, suddenly behind me, thumping my shoulder. His beady eyes dart around, never really landing on me. I don't answer. The noise of the room steadily creeps inside my skull. Rockabilly reminds me of somebody but I can't think who. A trickle of sweat runs down my side. Why don't I speak up?

"I'm counting on you, Doug. I know you can do this. Three minutes. That's it. You just gotta stay *up* for three minutes." He throws an arm around me, gives me a quick man-hug. "Okay?" I feel his hand in my pocket, slipping out the flask. My hip gives a warning twinge but I still don't speak up.

"You can do it, Dougie," Rosie adds, pulling me down to kiss my cheek. I step on the bucket and slip under the rope. The Punks in the room jump up and hoot and clap. I raise my hand in salute.

"Nice haircut," a fat cop says, nodding at my Mohawk. He's a moron and I try to think of something to say back, but I'm having trouble concentrating. Hot air blasts down from the fan whirling overhead.

"How old are you, son?" The cop's face gets way too close. Beads of sweat in the whiskers on his upper lip gross me out.

"Nineteen," I lie, like Mark said. "And I'm not your fucking son." The cop offers me a clipboard.

"Thank God for that. Sign here. Know the rules?"

I don't know shit about rules, but I scribble on the release form and nod. I can't take my eyes off Rockabilly; he's swelling up. One cop holds out boxing gloves. I shove my right hand in, then my left, feel my thumbs slide into pouches. Another cop talks; I see his lips moving but don't quite catch the words. I need to throw up. The beer?

Rockabilly holds his gloves out. I don't know what he wants me to do. He taps the tops of mine. I glance at Mark and Rosie, see them cheering. The noise is completely inside my head now, like a 747 taking off. I can't *think*. Cement seems to be filling my body, pressing against my lungs, squeezing my heart. For a quick sec, I go outside myself, see how I must look up here—six-four and 140 pounds, Black Flag T-shirt, ripped jeans, and engineer boots. Then Rockabilly winks and too late, I recognize who he reminds me of.

A bell sounds; Rockabilly circles to the left. I manage to turn to keep him in my sights, but he still clips me a good one. I stumble back a few steps, then swing. Miss. Turn around and swing again. Miss. The plane accelerates. I put up my arms. His fist jabs at my shoulder. His eyes crinkle, his lips stretch to a smile. He hits me harder, I trip over my own boot. I somehow connect with his jaw. He looks as surprised as I feel, then dances up and wraps his arms around me.

"Stupid. Asshole." He speaks slowly, over-pronouncing every word, hissing them into my ear. "Punk." His tongue flicks at my ear lobe. He pounds my kidneys, thrusts me off of him. I go to swing, but he's quicker. His fist lands so hard in my gut, the air rockets out and I collapse forward, folded over but still standing. I hear Rosie yell my name. Did I make it? Was that three minutes?

I try to straighten up; Rockabilly sends his other fist into my face. Impossibly sharp pain, like crystal shattering, I see/hear/feel my nose crunch. The room blurs. I fall in slow motion. Land with a jolt on hands and knees. My hip explodes. I imagine the metal pin giving way, the entire hipbone falling off, my leg connected to my body only by skin. Blood drips in steady rhythm from my nose to the mat. My face throbs. I can't breathe. Darkness rims my vision; stars appear.

"Had enough, Shithead?" He squats beside me. He's got that cop smile on his face.

The bastard knows I can't answer. I can't catch a breath.

"You didn't last two minutes, you stupid little shit."

My father's voice. My father's words.

I'm seven again, locked in the body cast. Ten, driving home from Henry's. Twelve, Carl on the floor because he tried to hit back. Helpless. Trapped. Like now. With no one to blame but myself.

My own *stupid* self.

I don't know how I come up off the mat or how Rockabilly stands up at the same time so my fist can meet his jaw with such force that he tumbles backwards into the rope. I *clearly* recall his face, the surprise as he bites hard on his tongue, leaks blood from his lower lip. How he raises his fists and tucks his head, curls his upper lip, stares back without blinking. How he dances back and forth, sneers and cusses and mouths ugly warnings.

He isn't smiling.

He'll show no mercy.

I don't care. At all.

Time is suddenly mine. Rockabilly continues to punch, but now I don't actually feel it. Brain function intensifies with each blow he lands—the moments separate and stretch so when he attacks, I see it coming like slow motion. I knock him down. Kick him in the butt.

"Mind the rules!" the referee shouts.

"Boot Party!" the Punks yell. I slam the heel of my boot into the small of his back.

One of the Punks that helped with the bikers tries to climb in the ring. Two cops snatch him down. Two more grab my arms and drag me back. The Punks are the ones smiling now. Rockabilly's on his knees, panting. I don't bother to call him names. He's small now, I don't need to. I hold up my arms and the crowd goes wild, even the jocks.

There is absolutely no noise in my brain except their applause.

I get a T-shirt and five grungy twenty dollar bills. I take the piss of a lifetime on the wall outside. Back in Mark's car, Rosie sits in the back with me and tells my story over and over again. At a liquor store, we pick up ice for my nose and Mark treats me to a six-pack of mixed drinks in a can. Manhattans. I guzzle one, then another. I like the bittersweet taste of the Coke and bourbon, how it backs off the pain and reminds me of Carl. Jack's girl sits on my other side. I let her hold the ice up to my nose.

"Social Distortion?" Rosie asks. "I think Dougie deserves it." She snuggles close, takes a sip of my Manhattan.

"Shit, yeah," Jack says. He's riding in front. He puts on Fear.

*"Let's have a war—Give guns to the queers!"*

I lean back and give over control to the music. Mark speeds across three lanes to take the exit for the 57. I rest on Jack's girl and she lets me reach up under her shirt. I am sixteen years old and this is the best day of my life.

## {3}

Slowly, I open one eye, close it again, and pull the covers up over my head. Way too much light—Mom's drawn back the drapes and opened one of the sliding windows. I hate mornings. I hate waking up. From outside, Frank Sinatra blasts on somebody's stereo, birds chirp and twitter, a lawnmower roars away, the Little League baseball brats sing *"Hey, batter batter!"* endlessly in the field behind our house, and some fool is pounding on a huge bass drum.

Except it's not a drum; it's my brain. Last night returns in a mass of jumbled images — Social Distortion, the Hells Angels, feeling boobs, Rockabilly. I smile at that part, remembering the glory of standing over him. How completely powerful it was. I touch my nose and gasp. Shit. Feels like a hundred slivers of glass sticking out of the side. I step over last night's clothes to peer into the mirror on my dresser. Both eyes look bruised. They'll be black before tomorrow. My nose takes up practically my whole face.

Was it worth it? The hundred vanished into Mark's pocket. He claimed he spent it all on pot, liquor, and Oki Dogs, mostly for me. Right. By the time we got to Irvine, Rosie copped an attitude and wouldn't talk to anybody. Jack's girl acted like I hadn't been feeling her tits the whole ride down. My face looked like meatloaf and felt like shit and I couldn't risk downing the rest of the Manhattans — too much campus security. Worst of all, Social Distortion *sucked*. Mike Ness was too wasted to sing or even stand up. He fell into Casey's drum set.

Wow. How Punk Rock.

"What the hell happened to you?" my father asks, snorting and shaking his head as I come downstairs. He's in his Saturday morning gardening outfit. Obviously taking a break. He probably worked a whole half hour, and now he's parked his fat ass in his easy chair, feet up, reading the *Tribune* and sipping a Heineken. The cat's curled against his leg. I cross through the living room to the kitchen.

"Hey! Asshole. I'm talking to you."

I stop at the kitchen door and pivot so he can fully take in the face. What's on the list today? We've covered how he hates the Mohawk and the way I dress, right down to the boots he doesn't even recognize as his. We know he doesn't work his ass off every day so I can piss away his hard-earned money. (No, Dad, I steal it, along with your cigarettes and booze. Use it in first period to buy Black Beauties from the hippie that sits in front of me.)

What now? I'm all ears, can't wait.

He stares, whistles, and rolls his eyes, doesn't even stand up. He shakes his head, snorts again, and goes back to his paper and beer. Smirking. More evidence that he's been right all along. I'm stupid, like all his kids; we can't do anything right. But I don't talk back like Chels or fight like Carl. I'm no fun to pick on. Maybe he knows I've gone as far as I will with him. Or maybe he's just tired out.

"Oh my dear God," Mom says when I go into the kitchen, her smile fading as she turns to greet me. She wipes floury hands on her apron and reaches up for my face. "What happened, Dougie?" She gently turns my face one way, then the other, and sighs.

"You should see the other guy."

"You got in a fight?" Her tone changes. She bustles over to the fridge and takes out the ice tray. "I've told you no fighting. I will not put up with—"

"No, Mom. No fight. I got smacked with the car door. Leaning down to pick up my wallet."

She stares like she can tell if I'm being honest. Nods. "Okay. Sit down. Let's get some ice on it." She hands me a couple of cubes wrapped in a dishtowel. She goes to touch it and I jerk away.

"Stop wiggling." She peers closer. "You need an X-ray." She sighs, glances toward the living room. "Your father will not be happy."

"So what else is new?" I ask.

She ignores me and chatters on. "Are you hungry? I have casserole, or I could fix you some eggs. What time did you get in?"

Blah blah blah. Dad belches and his chair creaks. The back screen door slams and the lawn edger starts up. I wonder where Rosie is. Why Social Distortion sucked so bad last night. What life means. If I have any pot left in my backpack. I try a bite of the cheesy chicken thing my mom puts in front of me, but the best I can manage is to let it melt down in my mouth. Chewing hurts. I need a cigarette, glance at the carton of Pall Malls shoved into the corner on the dish counter. Does Mom have any Darvon? The room gets still and I look up. Mom's glaring, eyebrows raised.

"Sorry. What did you say?" I ask.

She speaks like I can't understand English. "Home-work. Did-you-do-your-home-work?"

"Oh. Yeah. All done." Right.

"Chores?"

"When I get back, okay? I got rehearsal."

*     *     *

"Well, bust a bitch, what the hell happened to you?" Anne says when she opens the door, sees my face. She loves our music and lets us practice in the backyard. I smile; I love to hear her talk. With her leftover Texas accent, *hell* sounds like two syllables.

"Got in a fight," I say, coming through the door.

"You should see the other guy," Rosie pipes up, coming in from the living room. Craig's outside on the drum set, practicing. Anne takes out a cigarette, offers me the pack and some matches. I light hers, then mine.

"Well, sing it for me," she says. "That new one you been working on." Rosie smiles. I get the beat going and we find a pitch. The lyrics are still messy, but the point is clear—hippies got to go, the day belongs to Punks. Anne claps when we're done. Roy and Glenn show up a few minutes later, do the whole "what the hell happened to you" thing, then we sit down to plan the next weekend. Craig knows a guy that's having a yard party and wants us to play.

"It's out in Montclair," he says. Rosie and I look at each other and bust out laughing. The guys look at us strange. We laugh more, out of control. It's so weird how I have one life with school and the band, and a whole other one with Mark and Jack and the older Punks I know. Rosie crosses through both. Skinny little Rosie, with her big brown eyes. Sweet kitten girl except when you piss her off. She'll pee on the side of the road with the guys. Cry in my arms like a baby.

"What?" Glenn asks, looking at us both, still laughing.

"Montclair sucks, man," Rosie explains.

This is the best. Craig behind me, pounding out the tempo, Glenn on bass, Roy on guitar (such as it is—he still only knows a few chords—but at least he's not an asshole anymore); me and Rosie rocking out the new songs, doing our covers, sometimes just fooling around and making shit up. It doesn't take long to drop into that space, where the power coming up from inside is enough to float me across the whole damn world. My brain fuses, joins itself, exists in one whole piece, not fractured or darting about stupidly in some random order. I get it. I get it all. My heart races to match the beat and my whole body joins the dance. No pain, none at all, only rhythm and words, life and death, this sacred moment of *being right here*.

We play until Anne comes out with both hands held palms up.

"Guess who?" she says. It's the cops, of course. They show up every week, usually the same ones.

"I don't know how y'all 'spect the younger generation to find their voice in this world when y'all won't even let them play their music." She says this every week. When she's had a few, her accent gets stronger.

"Sorry, Mrs. Harris," he says. "Your neighbors—"

"Oh, I know about my frickin' neighbors! Don't you tell me about

my neighbors! They got one helluva lot of nerve. Y'all come by some
time when they're going at it—"

"We'd be glad to, you just call us."

"Y'all can bet your sweet patooties . . ."

"It's okay, Mom," Craig says. "We were about done anyway."

The cops leave. Anne goes to the refrigerator and brings back a six-
pack. Sets it down on the coffee table near where we're all lounging.

"Help yourself."

She does this every rehearsal. Says she'd rather have us drinking
here, where she can keep an eye on us. Good for her. She plops in her
chair and picks up her own drink. "Y'all are good kids, you hear me?
You are good kids."

"Thanks, Anne," Rosie says.

"I mean that. Y'all do some good playing too."

"Mom—"

"I'm not done, Craig." She sips her screwdriver. "You kids are artists
so there's something you better know. It's not an easy life. Not at all.
The world does not understand artists." She peers at each of us, one at
a time, ending with me. "You 'specially, Doug, you got something."
She wiggles her cigarette at me. "You're going to go far, young man.
You are going to go *far*."

## {4}

"Freaks."

This from a butt-ugly fat guy in a suit. Belly bulging over his pants.
Standing with his bald shithook buddy outside Long's. Jack sighs,
shrugs. We're not bothering anybody; we need cigarettes. Long's
happens to be the only store open. The two creeps stare like they
own the place, like they got the right to judge. We slow up and stare

right back. Jack hawks a good one into his hand, holds it up to his nose, and snorts it in. The bald guy gags and heads out into the parking lot. The fat one waddles behind him, muttering and shaking his head.

Inside, Jack goes to the counter to pick up the smokes. I head down the liquor aisle, snatch a fifth of JD and slip it in my coat pocket, smooth like, without slowing a step. I grab a Coke from the cold section and join Jack at the counter to pay for it. We head back to the street, our long gray trench coats flapping out. Mine's got FEAR spray-painted down the left and across the back. We're wearing peg-leg Levis, tucked into engineer's boots. Thrift store shirts. Choke-chain dog collars wrapped under and around the boots, with a lock. Rags too, red—mine's tied on my boots like a cowboy does his kerchief, Jack's is wrapped higher up around his leg. His hair's spiked now. I've got a buzz cut with a bleached-in W and Y—for Wasted Youth. I like how I look. I like walking with Jack. I like the feeling that we know who we are and aren't scared to say it.

We pile into Mark's old Chevy with Rosie and a shitload of other people, all Punk: flattops, tiny Mohawks, one of the girls with the cat-Mohawk combed straight back, the other girl with red spiked hair. Jack hands out smokes and Mark pulls away from the curb. We're going to Hollywood; clubs are half-priced on Tuesdays. I glance at the clock: just after ten.

"You feeling anything?" Rosie asks. I shake my head no. I down half my Coke and fill up the can with Jack Daniels.

"Shitty mushrooms, huh?" she sighs. "Shoulda known. You never get anything good for free."

The girl with the cat lights up a joint. She passes it around. Mark shoves Black Flag into the tape deck.

*"I'm going to explode!*
*I've had it!"*

"You okay?" I ask Rosie quietly. She leans over on me, speaks softly so only I hear, cuts her eyes towards Mark.

"My stepdad's home."

"Shit, sorry."

"Yeah." She never tells Mark what the asshole tries when he's there and her mom's at work. He'd go and kill the guy.

"Want me to come over?"

She nods and slips her hand into mine.

Just past eleven, we pull onto Sunset and go west. We stop at a light. The car next to us is one of those Baja Bugs with the big stinger thing in the back and the tail pipe that goes up. Stuffed with hippies. The driver revs his motor.

"What you looking at, asshole?" I say out my window.

"UP YOURS, weirdo," the passenger replies.

They're playing Devo—"Are We Not Men?" Mark sticks his finger in his mouth and pretends to puke. One of the hippies leans out the backseat passenger side and yells, "Punk sucks and disco swallows!" just as the light changes. They gun the car and zoom on ahead, laughing like the stupid shits they are. We catch up at the next red light.

"Don't, man, you'll get us in trouble," the girl with the cat says as we open all four car doors.

"Shut up," Rosie tells her. "We don't take shit, okay?"

The hippies try like hell to roll up their windows, but we're too quick. I grab the driver's side window when it's halfway up and press my whole weight on it, which hurts my hands but breaks the window. I kick the door and then punch out the creep inside. The Punks in the cars behind us are going crazy, cheering out their windows and honking. Rosie and cat girl are yelling too.

"Dirty stinking hippie," Jack says, and dukes the asshole in the passenger seat. His head flops and Rosie squeals. Jack hits him again. Mark kicks in the window in the backseat and gets one more good punch in before the light changes. We sprint back and jump in our car, ready to go around again at the next light except the chickenshits make a left at the corner.

"That'll teach them," Mark says. "They'll watch their mouth next time they come to Hollywood."

"*If* they come," Jack adds.

"Damn straight, man," I chime in. "It's our town now."

The Whiskey's got a line around the block but we go direct to the front door. We're here a lot and the skinhead bouncer gives us a nod. We sail on past some wannabe punk types and slide on in. I like being known. I like the skinheads. They don't take crap from anybody. Clubs hire them when Punk Rock's playing because so much wild shit happens. It's just how Punk is. People need to release. The more damage you do, the better you feel. No pretense. No posing. Pure aggression, that's Punk.

The second the inside door opens, the volume triples. My heart rate jumps to keep time with the music, which is inside and outside all at the same time. I'm filled up and surrounded, safe. I feel all of my body, down to my fingertips. I know who I am, what I can do, where I'm going, how to get there. I know something else too. I'll be here one day, playing my music. Saying my words. Being in charge. Like coming home.

A kid with tattoos all down the side of his face leaps on the stage. The bass player shoves him off. He scrambles up again, this time with a friend; a skinhead bouncer steps forwards, swings them back to the floor. The drummer kicks off the set. The guitars join in. A circle forms. Mark slips in and hunkers down, elbows pumping, starting to skank. Rosie hangs out by me. The circle grows bigger. Girls usually don't skank, it's too rough. Only the tuff bitches get in the pit—then complain how some guy grabbed their ass or tits or something.

I want to jump in but never have. Too damn dangerous. Stupid even. A guy goes down. His buddies reach in to get him on his feet. Fine. But what if there's no one you know? What happens then?

"Hey." Rosie elbows me in the ribs. I bend down to hear. "Over there. Check her out. She's been staring at you for five minutes."

I straighten to see an outrageous Punk chick across the room. Bleached blond hair, with that wide girl-style Mohawk, black-rimmed bright green eyes. She nods and purses her lips, looks back at the band. Rosie nudges me with her foot; she's watching Mark in the slam pit, pretending not to be with me. I hate how I'm stupid with chicks, unless they're my friends, but cross the floor anyway. I stand next to her and pull out my flask, gulp some and hold it out to her. Without taking her eyes off me, she accepts it and drinks. I don't talk. I turn back to watch the band. The singer's jumped onto the crowd. Three punks are up on the stage.

In between songs, she nudges me and points at herself.

"Stacie!" she yells up at me.

"Doug!" I yell back.

She grabs my hand and for a second I'm confused, until I figure out she's slipping me a pill. I wash it down with my whisky. Almost immediately my heart rate jumps even higher. Speed. Not usually a good choice for me, but too late now. I go with it. We hang out the rest of the night, until just before two, when we head outside. Mark and Rosie are already there, talking to people. The bouncers start moving us out. We head down Sunset.

"Hey," Mark asks, grinning, "anybody feel like a snack?"

"I need a pack of cigs," Stacie answers, her eyes twinkling.

"Let's do it," I say. The four of us and a Punk named Gene cross the street over to the Danny's Liquor. Me and Mark go in first. The chink at the counter flicks his squinty eyes back and forth, presses his lips together. Only one other person's in the store, an old man, checking out cough syrups. Counter guy can't decide what to do. Mark gives him a friendly nod and I hear him sigh. We stroll back to the cold drinks section. Stacie and Rosie come in a few seconds later, laughing, shaking their heads.

"We are bloody lost!" Stacie announces, pretending an English accent. "How do you get to the 405?"

The old man finally picks his syrup and lines up behind them. Rosie asks for a pen to write directions; so counter guy has to duck down. His eyes keep darting toward us and she keeps asking questions. She scribbles his answers on a paper bag.

"C'mon, c'mon!" the old man mutters, and coughs. "I'm dying here. I ain't got all night."

Gene comes in. Lines up behind the old guy.

"Could we hurry it up, ladies?" he says.

"Bug off, man," Rosie shoots right back.

"I need some smokes!" Gene says.

"C'mon, c'mon," the old man adds, coughing more.

Mark and me start for the door. We're packing beer and every kind of chip we could grab.

"HEY!" counter guy shouts. "Come back here. You got to pay!" He barrels around the counter and we all run. "HEY! You got to pay!" The old guy with the syrup steps up to the register. We fly across Sunset, dodging cars, and down Larrabee, boots thudding and chains jangling. A few blocks later, out of breath and laughing, we duck in the back of a carport behind an apartment complex. We crack open the beer. Talk about the bands. Laugh at how funny the chink looked.

"So where you from?" Stacie asks, later. She's leaning against me.

"La Verne," I say.

"No shit? I live in Pomona."

"I used to live there," I said, "Until the cholas took over."

"What are you talking about?" Rosie asks, laughing.

"You know, *cholas*. Mexican girls. Bitches tried to beat up my sister and my dad freaked out, so we moved. The whole neighborhood was going down, you know what I mean?"

"I'm half Mexican," Stacie says and I shut up, close my mouth. Mark starts to laugh.

"Way to go, Doug."

"Teasing," Stacie says, straightening her skirt as she stands. "I got to work tomorrow." She holds out her hand. "Want a ride home?"

We hike back up to Sunset and over to Tower Records to her beat-up old Punk-mobile. I'm back to not talking. We hit the freeway and listen to Fear. I find out she's twenty-one and has a job at 7-Eleven. That she thinks I'm sexy. I finish my flask. We exit and end up in a not-so-great area of Pomona. She parks in the alley behind a wooden apartment building. An argument is going on somewhere in Spanish. I check around, but don't see anyone. Mexican music blasts out of a car parked on the street.

I follow her up an outside flight of stairs and down the walkway. Her apartment's at the end. Inside, a surfer-looking chick is curled up asleep on the couch. "My sister," Stacie explains and leads me down a short hall to her room. Punk posters are all over the walls — the Germs, Sex Pistols, the Plugz, the Bags, Black Flag, and more. Mattress on the floor with a sleeping bag open on top. She lights incense and puts a Black Flag tape into the ghetto box on the dresser.

*"I'm about to have a nervous breakdown — my head really hurts . . ."*

"How old are you?" she asks, slipping off her leopard vest. She's not wearing anything underneath.

"Nineteen." Shit. Am I actually forming words?

She snorts. "Uh-huh." She drops her skirt and stands there in boots and panties. Boom — I'm hard. "So are you a virgin?"

"Of course not. Are you shitting me?" Fuck yeah I'm a virgin.

She drops her head forward and smiles up at me. "It doesn't matter. Come here."

I do. She kisses me and starts unbuckling my jeans. Can this be happening? She keeps talking and moving, kissing, touching. I lose track of all that's going on.

I don't do so good the first time.

She kisses me after, anyway. We go again and I start to get the way of it. *Real sex* is not at all like making out or doing it myself. Real sex is like I'm talking to God. Running the Universe. Everything possible. No wonder they don't want you do it—'cause after you find out about it, you don't want to do anything else.

\*     \*     \*

Stacie drops me off at school the next morning. Kisses me right there. I hear catcalls from the group of stoners and cheerleaders standing by the tree, preening like peacocks at the zoo in their ugly Izod shirts. I don't give a damn what anybody says to me today. I got laid last night. Nothing else really matters.

"Tonight?" she says. "I get home around seven. See you?"

I nod. Get out of the car feeling bigger than life. Ignore the stares and comments from the jocks. Strut across the grass, past the tree that sits in the front of the yard, catch up with Rosie near the quad. She smiles. She can tell.

## {5}

Me and Rosie pass the Barbies at the tree after school. It's their spot. They congregate every afternoon to check out people leaving campus. Today, they're in their little cheerleader outfits. Evelyn Anderson's right up front. I still have fantasies about her tits. Rosie notices me staring and pokes me with her elbow.

"Sorry," I mumble, but still look.

"Cute hair, Rose," one says. "Love the color."

"Yeah, what's that called?" says her friend. "Puke?"

"Fuck you," Rosie says.

"Oh! You rape my virgin ears!" Evelyn chirps. The Barbies bust out in giggles. Rosie rolls her eyes.

"Hate this school," she mutters.

"I know." I think about Evelyn in black leather. Dog collar around her neck. Me holding the chain.

"I'm gonna drop out, move in with Mark. Get high and do music. That's all. That's all I want to do."

"Sounds good, until they arrest him and put you in foster." I take the Marlboro Lights from my sleeve, offer her one.

"Not if we're famous first." She lights it, takes a deep drag and lets it out her nose. "We could be, you know. It happens."

We walk and smoke, stop to finish before turning onto her street. She sighs, loud and long.

"Ready?" I ask. She nods.

We stub out the smokes and she hands me a piece of peppermint gum as we go round the corner and up the walk to her apartment. She lives on the ground floor of a two-story, just on the edge of the city. Her face pales as she sticks the key in the front door. I hear her take a long slow breath. It's weird how many Punk girls I know have shit to deal with at home. Rosie's mom's okay, just never here, which is why Rosie's real dad and his new wife got the twins, who are five. He wanted Rosie too, but she didn't want to live in Sacramento, or leave her mom. The trade-off is the shithook stepdad, Frank. Who doesn't have a job.

He's in the living room when we open the door, reading a magazine, drinking a beer, getting fat. He grins when he sees Rosie; the grin fades when he notices me.

"Oh. Hey. Doug," he says, slapping the grin back on. "Good to see you. Where you been hiding, big guy? Want a beer?"

"Nope." As we planned, I settle on the couch as Rosie goes to change. She doesn't even look at him. The silence gets awkward quickly.

"So, guy, how's school?"

"Fine."

"The band?" He's still grinning.

"Good."

"You guys playing anywhere?"

"Uh-huh."

"Got any new songs?"

I nod, but don't speak. I pull my switchblade from my back pocket and pick at my fingernails. He shifts in his chair. His mouth moves like he's going to say something, but he doesn't. His eyes dart around, he nods to himself, and with one last nod at me, goes back to reading the magazine. I stare relentlessly.

"What?" he asks, a few minutes later. I don't move, just keep staring. "For Christ's sake, Doug," he blurts, slamming the magazine down. "What's your problem today?"

"I have no problem." There's sweat on his upper lip. "You do. You have a big problem, Frank."

I see him watching the blade. Getting still. "What are you saying?"

"You need to leave Rosie alone."

Bright red spots appear in his cheeks. He sets his magazine down. "I don't know what you mean."

"Plain English. Is that hard for you, Dumbass?" My father's words. "Leave Rosie the fuck alone."

He stands; I'm there before he can take a step, towering over him by at least six inches. With an open knife. He sits back down.

"Doug, really, if you're implying . . . I mean; come on, that's just ridiculous—"

"Frank, Frank—do I look stupid to you?" My father again. I like how it feels.

"No, Doug, of course not. Not at all. But this is definitely some sort of a misunderstanding. I mean, come on, I would never—"

There's a snort from Rosie as she appears at the end of the hall. Frank's cheeks get redder.

"Good to know." I pick out some dirt from under my thumbnail, flick it onto the rug. "'Cause Rosie's got some crazy-ass friends." I run the blade alongside my cheek, sharp edge on skin. "We don't like to worry about her."

Rosie steps into the room, comes to stand by me. I slip my arm over her shoulders.

"What do you think, huh? Frank? Should we be worried?"

He looks from her to me, wets his lips. "No, not at all. Nothing to worry about. I swear."

"Wow, like that's really good to know. Frank. 'Cause if I heard anything, you know, like *anything* . . ."

"You won't."

With my free hand, I close up my knife, slide it back in my pocket. "So that's that, huh?" I look down at Rosie. "Ready?" She nods and we head out the door. We saunter down the block without looking at each other.

The second we turn the corner, we burst out laughing.

"Oh my God. You are amazing!" She pulls her cigarettes out of her purse, taps one from the pack. "I think he shit his pants." Her hand's shaking as she tries to light it. I take the match and do it for her.

## {6}

Jenna Boston makes my dick hard just by walking past, which she's done several times during this set. It's our first paying gig—Jenna's nineteenth birthday. Anne is friends with Jenna's mom; she arranged it all. We're outdoors, up in the really fancy homes on Blue Bird Hill. Me and Rosie are rocking out. Even Roy's doing good. Great yard, tons of people, most of them loving it. Not many Punks, except for Jenna, who's fresh cuts, but she's got a flair. She's also got huge tits. My weakness. I screw up a lyric and Rosie shoots me a look.

On our break, we head to the cooler for beer.

"You better watch that shit," Rosie says.

"What?" I hold my palms up.

She glances to where Jenna's approaching. "I'm not stupid, Doug."

"Yeah, well, you better not be a big mouth either."

"Hey, thanks for coming," Jenna says, totally ignoring Rosie.

"No problem." I crunch up my beer can and grab a fresh one. Rosie snorts.

"You staying the whole time?" she asks. "I mean, after you play?"

"Are we invited?" Rosie says.

Jenna still doesn't change her gaze. "Of course you are." Her tongue darts to touch her upper lip.

"So, Doug, is Stacie coming by?" Rosie says in a challenging tone.

"No, she's working," I say.

"Who's Stacie?" Jenna asks. She finally looks at Rosie.

"My sister." I catch Rosie's eyes, briefly. She holds her hand by her face with the middle finger pointing up, then goes to talk with Craig and Roy. The thing we all know is, Jenna sleeps around. No reason why I shouldn't take advantage of it. Stacie won't care. Especially if she doesn't find out.

"Cool." Jenna moves a little closer and a dark-haired jock type marches over, like he's in charge of something. He snatches her arm, pulls her away. He's wearing a light blue Izod shirt. I hate Izod shirts.

"What are you doing?" he demands.

"None of your business, Brian," Jenna says, snatching her arm away. "Don't be a prick."

"Don't you be a bitch then." He grabs her again. I step between so that he has to go through me to get to her.

"Back off, dude," I say.

"That's my girlfriend, asshole," he says, slurring a lot.

"Like hell," Jenna says.

"Leave it alone, huh?" I hate this guy already. "Make this easy."

He blinks once, knocks the beer out of my hand. Reaches for Jenna again. She steps back. He lurches forward.

"You don't want to do this, Brian." I say his name with emphasis, making it special. He tries to punch me in the face. It's way too easy to avoid him. I clock him on the head, open-handed. He's not worth bruised knuckles. I doubt he feels it; he's too drunk. People move in to watch. Craig and Rosie come up beside me.

"Let's just play, all right?" Craig says.

"Exactly what I'm trying to do."

"Come on then," Rosie adds, but when I turn, Brian pushes me, like a girl would. I whirl and deck him. This time I use my fist. He lands on his butt in a bush. His nose starts to bleed. I shake my hand. That hurt! He stumbles up, rushes me, but all I have to do this time is get out of the way and let him trip on my leg. He sprawls out on the ground.

"Doug," says Rosie, grabbing my arm, pointing. Four cops stand in the driveway.

"All right. What's going on here?"

We find out later the neighbors called because of the noise. My luck they arrived just then. The cop in front scans the yard. Where do his eyes land? Me and Brian. He starts toward us, buddy in tow, Wyatt Earp and Doc Holiday marching to the OK Corral.

Craig whispers, "Great."

Brian's a jock, I'm a Punk Rocker. We all know what happens next.

"Hey, bud, what's that you got there?" a cop asks me from behind. Some secret signal goes out and suddenly guns are up and pointed directly at me. Like fucking Starsky and Hutch.

"He's got a weapon!"

"All of you—get your hands on your heads!"

The cops are all yelling and everybody puts their hands up, except Brian, who's pretty much out of it. I stand perfectly still, slowly lock my fingers behind my head, keep Rosie in my sight. I'm not looking to be in the obituaries because somebody thought I was trying something. The cop pulls my switchblade out of my back pocket. It's closed, I haven't used it, had no plans to, but it's there. That's all they need.

"The rest of you—over there," one cop orders.

The party's busted and with it, my chance of getting laid. Brian's twenty-two and in an Izod shirt, so he gets a lecture about "Drunk and Disorderly," then a ride home. I get arrested. All my stuff's at Stacie's, so I lie and say I'm nineteen. I don't really care if I have to go to jail; I do not want my parents knowing about it. Rosie'll call Mark and he'll get me out. Meantime, I'll just be cool.

All the way downtown, the cops in the front seat make fun of my hair, my clothes, anything they can think of. At the jailhouse, my stuff is checked in. I strip and my clothes are taken away in a plastic bag. A cop sizes me up, bends me over and makes me spread my cheeks. I'm ready to hit him if he touches me, but he doesn't. I put on an orange jump suit and get a brown paper sack with a baloney sandwich on

white bread, potato chips, and a runt-sized apple. A different cop puts
me into a holding cell with a old man puking all over himself. He leers
up at me when he's done. He's missing two teeth; his breath could
start a riot.

I was wrong about my I.D. I'd stashed it in the bottom of my backpack. When this is discovered, the troops return.

"You're in *tenth grade*?" says the cop who takes me out, brandishing
my school I.D. card. He obviously knows the answer; what's the point
in answering? Children's Services shows up. A social worker takes me
to a cubicle where she asks a bunch of stupid questions like did the cops
treat me okay, tells me not to worry, my parents are on their way, and
advises me not to say anything to the police without my mom or dad
there. She and a cop walk me past puking guy to a cell all my own.

I have to pee but the toilet's almost completely exposed to the room
so I figure I'll just hold it. But no one comes and finally I just bite it and
piss away. This is all Brian's fault. I start writing new lyrics in my head:

*Kill preppies, kill preppies, die!*
*Vomit on the clothes they wear—*
*Stinking up all the air!*
*They're just a bunch of fuckin' fags!*
*Their chicks are always on the rag!*
*Kill preppies, kill preppies, DIE!*

Finally, a cop unlocks the cell door and leads me down to an office, my
hands cuffed behind me. I can see my mom and dad in profile through
a huge office window, sitting stiffly in chairs facing a desk. A stern-
faced black cop is talking. My mother's expression is cold and tight,
like when she first came back from seeing Carl in the hospital. No
smile. My dad looks at the floor.

My parents don't like whatever the cop's saying. He sets a paper in front of them both. They sign it. I'm led into the office. They all stand and turn toward me, six-feet-four in an orange suit, suddenly feeling like I'm three years old. The handcuffs are removed. My father glares at me but my mother won't look. They wait while I change back to street clothes, again with the social worker there. She talks to my mom as my dad and I go to the property room to get my stuff.

The walk through the parking lots takes forever.

"They got your name, now, Douglas," my mom says, in a low scary tone. She still won't look at me. "You'll have no more chances. None."

"Stupid fucking move there, Asshole," Dad says, not yelling but in that voice where he might as well be. "Real fucking stupid."

I feel myself shrink. I fight it.

"Well, Asshole? What do you have to say for yourself, huh?"

"I didn't fucking do anything."

He turns and smacks me, the one and only time. It isn't hard, a slap to the side of the head, but I get tears anyway. I make sure he doesn't see. "You watch your mouth in front of your mother."

I get in my dad's BMW.

Orange, like the one that hit me.

I think of David Steele. I feel exactly like I did lying on the floor trying to get my breath after Rockabilly punched me in the gut. I think of how good it would feel to punch my father's face and see the surprise as he drops.

{7}

"Tonight, Doug. You got to. You need to get all that crazy shit out of you." Me and Stace are at the Cuckoo's Nest down in Costa Mesa. I've been staying at her place. I have to. My parents think they can still get away with grounding me. They're deluded, both of them. It's way too late for parental discipline. One day into it, I pack a couple of bags and head out the door.

"You go, you don't come back," my dad threatens.

I hold up my finger and keep walking.

"Asshole," he yells.

"Prick," I call back.

X is playing, screaming out the lyrics:

"... *we're desperate, get used to it* ..."

The club's got these great big wire spools for tables—people are rolling them all over the place. It's wild. A punk tries walking on one like those loggers on TV. Bouncers move in. Finally, they clear the space. People circle up, start to skank.

Skanking is unreal.

People hunker down really low, everybody in big ass boots with razors and kilts on over jeans. They start out like they're running in slow motion, then go faster and faster. They throw out elbows, punching whoever's in the way, moving things along. They make mean faces. They come onto people and roll over their backs. More people join up and they get going fast. I'm breathing hard, like I just had sex. I can't turn away. But I still can't make myself go in.

What wrong with me? I'm Punk. I am totally and thoroughly PUNK. I got the clothes, the hair, the attitude. What's my problem? What the hell am I waiting for?

Stacie gives me a little shove. A wink. She bumps me with her butt. "You got to do it, babe," she says. "You need to."

She's right. I can't be half-ass anymore. That's my parents' generation. I have to walk my talk.

I squat down as far as I can, lean forward. I edge around the circle and play follow-the-leader, moving my arms back and forth. I feel like an idiot at first, like I'm not doing it right. I keep on anyway. Nobody's judging. We're in it together. I stick my elbows out and the guy behind me gets it in the nose. That's just how it is. Round and round we go, like a training march. Like boot camp. Like I'm part of an army. Doing some badass tribal march. Powerful. Grounded. Intact. No words needed.

Somebody stomps on my foot. Somebody elbows me in the side of the head. It doesn't matter; I can take it. I even like it. The guy in front of me falls and I step over him. I don't know him so I don't stop. I don't hate him or anything, I just don't need to help him up. The music swells. It's bigger than the universe and faster than life. It's inside me and it surrounds me, all at the same time.

My life is good.

# Late 1978

A YEAR AND A HALF BEFORE

SAN FRANCISCO

{1}

Fisherman's Wharf is jumping tonight. The drummers are out in front of Ghirardelli Square, rocking their beat as the hippies dance. Across the street from where the cable cars turn around, the Buena Vista blasts Donna Summer:

*"Let's dance — this last dance — tonight!!!"*

Tommy grabs my hand and whirls me once in his best disco turn. I throw my head back dramatically and laugh like crazy. I catch the eye of some fat cow of a woman getting off the cable car. Probably from Wisconsin. She scowls. I wink. She whispers something to her fat cow husband. Usually, this would freak me out. Tonight, I do not care. I throw both arms around Tommy and plant one right on his lips.

I don't sleep with Tommy, but we're close, like Davy and me might have been if it weren't for our mom. He takes care of me. Today, he treated me to lunch — clam chowder in a sourdough bowl, my fave — and we spare changed a bit, using the story about being brothers with a dad who OD'd. The day was hot but the weather now, early evening, is warm, with a tiny breeze. Clouds on the horizon, like there could be one of those summer rains. Beautiful and perfect. Even the fog, which lingers along the mountain, is waiting its turn.

"So what are you going to be when you grow up?" Tommy asks, licking around the ice cream cone he just bought.

"An actor," I say. I stick the top of mine in my mouth. "I'm going to have my own TV show."

"Me, I want to be rich," he says. "*Filthy* rich. With a yacht and a big house in Tiburon, on the Bay." He glances at his watch. "Ooopsie. Shall we?"

The cable cars look impossible, too many tourists, but we squeeze on anyway and ride to the end of Powell. No charge. We hop off and walk down Market to Zim's. Nick and Adam are already eating dinner. They got some time to kill before they go to work.

"Sure you don't want to come?" Nick teases, as he fixes his hair a bit. I'm holding the mirror.

"I keep telling you — I'm not a whore."

"Neither am I," Nick snaps, takes the mirror from my hand. "I'm a businessman."

"Bitch, please," Adam says, waggling his French fry in my face. "You do the same thing for free." He takes a delicate last sip of milkshake.

"That's different." I dab a fry into the ketchup.

"Oh. Right. I forgot," Adam says, making a prissy face. "*You* get breakfast."

I smack him and we all laugh. They head back to Polk. Tommy has to go check on a new kid he met. I hang out to spare change, and make twelve dollars right off the bat, almost enough for food tomorrow. Good day. I smile, thinking of Fisherman's Wharf. I wonder where Tommy is, if any of the boys are getting a room tonight. I'm about ready to head back over to check on them when a cop in a black-and-white pulls up. Double parks. Rolls down the window.

"Hey, kid," he calls, "where are you headed?"

"Home," I say. Why didn't I see him? I glance each way, there's no place to run. He gets out, comes over to the sidewalk. He's cute. Really cute.

"It's pretty late," he says, checking up and down the street. "Where do you live?"

"Um, I, uh, in the East Bay?" Shit. Why don't I lie?

"You know, son, we have curfew laws in San Francisco. I'm going to have to call your folks. Come on." He whips out handcuffs and I turn around, put my arms behind me.

"No, that's okay," he says. He puts the cuffs on in front, not tight, and escorts me over to his car, holding my elbow with one hand, his other hand on my shoulder. He opens the front door, not the back. I slide in.

I'm inside a real cop car. It's amazing. Lights and a computer right in the car! A radio that keeps buzzing and talking. I should be scared, but all I can think is — how cool. Like I'm on a TV show or in a movie, with a cop so cute he really could be an actor. His nametag says MALONE. I start planning how to describe him to Tommy.

He doesn't say anything else, not to me. He nods once and I smile. Does he think I'm cute too? Hard to tell. He makes a couple of calls on his radio and we go to the station down on Bryant, where the jail is. We drive through a tall steel gate that rolls shut behind us. A police van is unloading a whole bunch of people, most of them either drunk or cussing. He waits until it's clear, then leads me to a desk inside. I sit on a metal chair.

"Well, son, what's your name?"

I tell him.

"Your parents' names? Home phone?"

"Just my mom." I tell him the number and remember how she worries about midnight calls.

"You okay?" the cute cop asks, dialing.

I nod — I really am okay. I'm great, actually. I just now realized that when a cop brings you home, your mom can't tell you to stay away. I'm going home. I'm going to have a bath in a tub and see Marianne and Davy and I can make up and —

"Mrs. Commagere? This is Officer Malone from the San Francisco Police. I've just picked up your son Jason." (pause) "No, he's fine." (pause) "We need to transport him back to you, so if you could — excuse me?" (long pause, cute cop glances over at me and my heart skips a beat) "Yes. Okay. What's the address?" He scribbles, I glance over — it's not any place I recognize. Did they move? "We'll see you in about 45 minutes."

Officer Malone doesn't cuff me this time. That summer rain shows up — it starts as we head south on the 101. We cross the Dumbarton Bridge. Again, we don't talk. I'm not quite so giddy anymore, because I don't know what's happening. We pull up in front of a house I don't recognize. A sign on the gate says DR. JEFFREY INGULSRUD, FAMILY COUNSELOR.

My mom's therapist. My heart races.

Is this where they hook you up to electrical wires to make you stop being gay?

"It's okay, son," Malone says, his hand now firmly on my shoulder. My knees wobble as we walk up to the porch. The cop knocks once on the door and an old bald guy with a scruffy beard opens it. He looks like the absent-minded professor.

"I'm Dr. Ingulsrud," he says. "Please come in."

It's pouring now, like it does in movies when bad things are about to happen. We wipe mud off our feet before entering. Dr. Ingulsrud doesn't look at me, just at my mom, who stands toward the back. She's perfect, as always, even in the middle of the night. Her hair's up and neatly pinned. She's wearing a yellow shirt tucked into black pants. She doesn't look a bit wet. She doesn't smile or speak, just smokes her cigarette and drops the ashes in a cup on the little table. I check around for the wires but see nothing. The doctor goes to her, leans down and whispers. She nods and finally looks over at us.

"Jason, come with me," she says. Her voice sounds natural and good. Maybe this will turn out all right. "Officer Malone, will you please stay? I won't be long."

"Sure."

Maybe she's sending me to Juvie, like she did Paul. Not much I can do about it now. Officer Malone smiles and gives me a slight nudge. I follow my mother into a room that used to be a bedroom, but now has only a table, a couch, and a chair. The doctor trails; he still hasn't looked at me.

No wires here, either.

"Call me if you need me." He pats her arm and leaves.

My mother stands facing me, arms crossed. She does not smile. She wears no expression at all; even her eyes are blank. My arms hang at my side. I'm having a little trouble breathing. My skin's prickly. I want to cry but something won't let me. I stand as still as I can and wait.

"Well?" she asks, and now her eyes are like lasers; boring into me.

I won't let myself look away. "Well, what?" She wants me to be scared, and I am. But I'm not going to let her see it.

"You have something to say to me?"

I press my lips together. I shake my head no. She wants me to ask her forgiveness. But for what?

"Nothing??"

She wants me to beg her to let me come home.

"I don't get it, Jason. You make that cop drag me out of bed at this ungodly hour of the morning and you have nothing to say?"

"No." Nothing she wants to hear.

"Has anything changed?" Her eyes flash, worse than the night she put me out.

"Like what?" I match her tone, best I can.

"Are you still a fag?"

It's like being punched where it makes you not able to breathe. I can't talk. My mouth drops open. I have to let the word hang there. I need time to fully take it in. Finally, I take a deep breath and speak.

"I'm still gay, if that's what you mean."

*This is when it happens.*
*This is what I will forget.*

My mother too takes a long, deep breath. Her head jerks. She steps away from me, puts a hand on the doorknob, turns again to stare. Her voice drops deep into her body.

"No child of mine is a faggot."

She waits. Is it a second or a year?

"Do you understand? You are not my son. I DON'T HAVE A FAG-GOT FOR A SON."

I think of dogs growling.

Of snails being crushed under shoes.

"Good for me then." I make my voice every bit as cold as hers. "Good for me."

"What did you say??" Deadly.

A blink. "I said — good."

Our eyes lock, the world goes away.

"Fag," she whispers.

"Fuck you."

She expands like a nightmare monster, growing eight feet tall in an instant and swooping down on me. I see her hand swing back so I close my eyes. She slaps me so hard in the face, my head whips around and I fly into the wall behind me. I see stars and scramble up anyway. I try not to cry but tears come; I don't know how to hold them back. She stares at me, her green eyes burning into my brain. As much as I want to, I can't look away.

She blinks once, slowly, and just a hint of a smile flickers across her face. Suddenly, she's a stranger to me, someone I've never even met. She turns, walks through the door, and gently closes it behind her.

It doesn't completely shut.

Through the crack, I peek to the other room. She lights a cigarette, her hands shaking. Mine are too. She starts to cry. The therapist puts an arm around her, pats her shoulder. Officer Malone glances toward the door, then puts his hand on her other shoulder. They all start to talk, low and intense. I can't hear the words, but I know what they're planning. Malone glances again.

I know what I have to do.

I shut the door and quietly push the button to lock it. My whole body's shaking now. I can barely crawl through the old sash window. I scratch my arm on a nail and see it start to bleed, but don't feel the cut. I drop to the ground and move as quick as I can, staying in the trees alongside the road, making it harder for them to follow. I look for the railroad tracks we saw coming out. If I can find them, I can find my way.

*How do I know this?*

There they are! I fly along them and round a bend and in this instant, know exactly where I am: these are the tracks where Davy, Paul, and I used to play, they're only a mile from the old house. I find the street. I go almost the exact path I took that first night, down to the train, to BART, passing St. Anne's.

At the station, I stand in the shadow of the pillar over on the side where the train will stop. I pray I haven't missed the last train. I stand straight, not touching anything. The rain's stopped. I don't know how long I wait. My legs tremble slightly from the running. Someone speaks to me, a guard? I stare at him; he shakes his head and blows air out of his mouth and moves away.

My body slowly disappears; my hands, my head, my face, gently drifting, like fog in wind. The train pulls in and I watch myself walk through the door, find a seat. I sit straight, upright, alone in the car. I don't move. I don't look out the window. I blink and we go down under the ocean. I feel? hear? the click-clacking on the tracks; it wraps around me, keeps me in place. I blink and watch myself climbing the stairs up out to the city.

Market Street's empty, like the first night. I go a block and then, suddenly, my body returns and I cannot walk one more step. I'm too heavy with pain I have no way to describe except that it seems to have soaked into every cell. I duck into an alley to lean against the wall, stare into — what? There is no city anymore.

No sky.

No lights or trees.

No stars or buildings.

I am connected to nothing.

A cricket chirps.

A breeze touches my cheek.

I draw in air — once, then again. How long have I been standing? A stray dog sniffs my fingers and I look down at him, scraggly and skinny. He dips his muzzle under my hand and peers up with his sad, dark dog eyes. I stroke his head a few times. He licks me once and trots off down the street. Somehow I manage to push myself up off the wall. It's the hardest thing I've ever done.

I put one foot forward, then the other. I don't see what's around me. I'm not sure when I end up at Dolores Park, or why I find a corner to huddle in. Why I take out my green sweater to wrap around my shoulders when I don't feel cold. I blink and watch Tommy and Nick come across the grass. Nick says words but I'm not getting them. Tommy hunkers down and gathers me in, holds me, rocks me. He strokes my face with his hand.

I don't feel it.

How could I? I don't really exist.

I'm only the skin that binds me together and the bones that hold me up.

# 1979

ONE YEAR BEFORE

LOS ANGELES COUNTY

Definitely boys' night out. Mark, Jack, and me are in Mark's car with a shitload of guys, heading to Cathay de Grande in Hollywood, to see African Dogs. The lead singer, Tony, is a friend of ours. Rosie's on a trip to see her dad in Sacramento and Stacie's hanging out with some old friends. Probably her ex-boyfriend Carlos from Argentina is one of them. Maybe she *is* half-Mexican. She sure as hell doesn't mind being around them. I don't care — Tony's probably going to ask me up on the stage tonight. I'm damn sure ready to sing in a club. The band's okay, but we're wasting our time doing yard parties. We need to move forward. I have to get my life going.

"I'm getting laid tonight," Mark announces, passing me the O.J., which is, of course, half vodka.

I stare at his profile as I drink. He's got to be at least twenty-seven now, if not older, and all he hangs out with are teenagers.

"That's messed up, man." I settle back and drink.

"You should talk." He cranks up Black Flag.

"That's way different. Stacie's older." *And probably with Carlos right now.*

"Yeah, well, what Rosie don't know ain't gonna hurt her." The car pulls up to the curb. He yanks the brake, leers at me, climbs out.

I'm drunker than I thought and stumble when I get out of the car, go down to one knee. Mark laughs. I shove him into the bougainvillea along the sidewalk. He scratches his hand on the thorns and comes running at me, body slams me into his car, starts my hip throbbing.

"Fuck you, man," I say, shoving him again. I hate how my goddamn hip interferes with everything. I stomp off down the street, trying not to limp. He tosses a rock that hits me in the back of my head and the cut bleeds a little onto my shirt. I flip him off without turning around, take out my flask, and down it.

"Sorry, man, you gotta be eighteen." The bouncer at the door stops me. "Let me see the license."

"Dude, it's way back in the car. I never bring shit here."

"Sorry. Need that I.D."

Tony sees me just in time, writes our names on the guest list and ushers me in. He takes me backstage to meet the rest of the band. I wait for them to invite me to sing, but he rambles on and on about some guy that wants them to sign a record contract. He goes to finish unloading and I head back to the main room. Mark and them come in but now I don't even care about them. I keep my distance. When the African Dogs get going, it occurs to me I could do as good as, if not better than, Tony.

*"Animals walk on all fours — rending talons crushers."*

Stupid lyrics. I jump in the circle to skank. Skanking is second nature already, feels like coming home. I focus on the bodies in front of me, on staying up and taking the blows as they come. My head mellows as the music and my heartbeat amp up. Around and around we go. I am finding my place, knowing where I am. Dancing with my tribe, in sync with my soul.

From out of nowhere, Tony lands on my shoulders, holding the mic, singing away. I grab his legs to keep him steady. We wail around the place, swerving and knocking into people, going the wrong way, turning around. He does something—grabs the wall, or maybe hits the ceiling with his head, I don't know—and he starts to fall. I hold on to his legs, too wasted to figure out why not just let go, so I fall with him. I split my chin open on the stage. Tony disappears. Mark pulls me up so I don't get trampled.

"Where the hell is Stacie?!" I yell, forgetting she didn't come.

Mark moves me to the side. He's laughing like crazy. "Ah, man, what an idiot, dude, that was hysterical."

I don't think; I hit him. He hits me back. In seconds, this blossoms to a full-on brawl. Bouncers move in and the next thing we know, we land on the street in front of the club. Not just me and Mark, but all the people we came with, plus some. I taste blood.

"Don't come back," the bouncer says.

"Man, this is your fault, Doug," Jack says. Mark's bleeding from his mouth. Looks like he cut his lip with his tooth.

I lift my middle finger.

"We're going," Jack announces and starts toward the street with our car. Mark and the rest trail after. Not one looks back.

"Who needs you?" I yell, wiping my mouth and getting blood all over my sleeve. My chin's got a gash down the side and there's a hole where my tooth used to be. I stumble to the edge of a planter, still totally smashed. They turn the corner. I could catch up if I went now.

I don't and minutes later, they drive past. Mark flips me off. I return the favor but now I've got no way home. I try to think when Stacie will be back so she can come get me, but then I can't remember her phone number. So what. I'll just sit here, see what happens.

A car stops in the middle of the street, the Dead Kennedys blasting from inside. A guy waves. I recognize him, but can't call his name.

"Need a ride?" he yells.

I cross Hollywood Boulevard—not easy at this time of night—and climb in the backseat. We go down to Oki Dogs for something to eat. My chin throbs but it's nothing compared to inside my mouth. The nerve must be exposed. I can't eat anything, I can't even open my mouth. Somebody has vodka and I chug it straight. My shirt's bloody. I wish I knew where Stacie was. I wonder if I could get ahold of Carl. The guys are going out to Claremont to a party but I don't want to. I know how to get home, I don't need anybody's help. I wait for the bus on the bench outside Oki Dogs. I spit a gob of blood and look around.

This street sucks. Too many faggot whores, walking around in their stupid tight pants and acting like they got a right to be here. Assholes. It's got to be obvious that I'm no faggot, but cars still slow down and check me out.

"Fuck you, queer!" I yell at one of them; he speeds away.

A Mercedes pulls up. I'm ready to cuss him too, but when he rolls down the window, he doesn't look gay.

"You okay, man?" he asks. "You need a ride?"

"No, man. I'm cool." Talking hurts.

"Quite a gash you got there," he says. "Want me to take a look? I'm a doctor."

"Fuck off."

"Bit of a bad mood, are we?" He chuckles a little. "Are you sure, now? It looks like a pretty deep cut. I've got my bag in the back."

I don't answer. He backs the car to right in front of the bus bench. "I've got something I can put on it, it might help."

I'm trying to wrap my brain around this but I'm not doing so good and suddenly notice his pants are unzipped. His dick is sticking straight up. He's holding himself, jerking off.

"Why don't I just come over there and fill up that hole for you?" he says, yanking faster, starting to pant.

I bash in the side of his door with my boot and manage to bend his antenna straight back before he gets it together to drive. I grab the trash can to throw at him, but it's chained to the bus bench so all I do is hurt my hand. A couple of faggots on the other side of the street start to laugh. I march toward them; they scatter. Now my hand hurts as well as my face.

Back at the bus stop, I won't sit down again. I pace until the bus finally shows up. I sit in the way back, across from a kid who reminds me of myself, two years ago, with his mean face on, looking stupid. We go down Santa Monica Boulevard and everywhere I look there's some faggot whore. Young kids, old queens, like cockroaches spilling out of bars. They kiss right there, on the street, groping each other. Makes me want to puke.

This whole city sucks. The air's poison, nobody gives a shit about anyone else. Everybody's out for their own. Get in the way and you're toast. The whole country's going down. You barely see a white face anywhere.

The bus lumbers to the stop closest to Stacie's and I hoof it over, my jaw hurting with each step. She's home when I get there, alone with her sister, watching some old horror flick. She takes one look my face and goes for the Mercurochrome. Makes me rinse with salt water and finds oil-of-cloves for my tooth. She hands me something from a prescription bottle and I take three, then one more for good measure.

I am so damn tired of getting beat down.

# 1979

## ONE YEAR BEFORE

## SAN FRANCISCO

## {1}

"Okay. You win. I'll do it."

"No shit?" Nick mumbles, mouth full of burger. "You serious?"

"Yeah. Why not, huh?"

It's not like I haven't been thinking about it for months, and the second the words are out, it feels right. It's time. I'm tired of begging and digging through garbage. I don't know why I've waited so long. Like Adam says — I do it for free anyway.

Adam shakes his head with amazement; Tommy grins; the new kid, Brandon, just stares. Was I ever that stupid?

"Let's go, okay?" I stand up. Now that I've made up my mind, I want to get it over with, I want the first time behind me.

"Look sexy," Tommy instructs, "and do not go anywhere with anyone until you see my signal." I got the crash course on the way to Polk Street. Now he ducks into a doorway with Adam nearby and pretends he's cleaning his nails.

I sit on the bench. I smile at cars. I drop my head slightly and peer up from under my long lashes. I'm cool until a car finally slows down, then I almost chicken out. The guy doesn't even fully stop. Why didn't he? What's wrong with me? A couple of old ladies drive by just then, the tight-faced one shakes her head at me. I flip her off.

"At least I'm not ugly," I yell, and hear Tommy laugh.

Not even a minute later, a dirty white Dodge Dart pulls over and stops. Is this it? Another huge breath. The guy has dull brown hair and keeps looking around like he's being followed. My stomach tries to jump out of my body, but I feel Adam smirking, so I pull myself together. We're the same age and he does this all the time. If he can, I can. It's just like being onstage, playing a character that isn't you.

I saunter over, lean on the car, peek down through the window. Sweat dots the guy's forehead and outlines his armpits, which grosses me out, but he doesn't smell, so that's good. His car is tidy, a briefcase in the back. I glance to my right; Tommy's watching. He scratches his nose with his thumb pointed *up*. It's a go.

"What will you do?" the guy asks, almost in a whisper. I'm about to answer, but remember to wait. When he doesn't say anything right away, I get nervous. He clears his throat. "And how much?" I relax. Cops can't ask — that's entrapment.

"Twenty for hand only. Forty if you want both." I can't believe how much I sound just like Nick or Adam. Like I'd been doing this forever.

"How much if I want to —"

"I don't do that." Good — cold, like I take no shit.

"But —"

"I don't do that."

I move away from the car, like Tommy told me, thinking the guy'll split, but he doesn't. He backs up, leans over again.

"Okay. That's okay," he says and swings the car door open. "It's fine, really, just fine." I get in.

It's happening.

I shut the door but keep my hand on the handle, so I can jump out if he tries to lock it. I'm surprised how clearly I'm thinking.

"Um, I want both. Where should we, um — ?" he mumbles. He doesn't look at me directly. I point around the corner, like Tommy said. We don't talk. He bumps the curb as he parks. Sweat glistens on his top lip. Still not looking at me, he unzips his pants.

Twenty minutes later, I step out with four ten dollar bills and he drives away. Tommy strolls up, grinning.

"See?"

I do three more that night, hand only. One guy cheats and gives me a ten but I don't notice till after. Nobody's mean and nobody's too gross. By the end of the night, I've made ninety dollars! Tommy stays close the whole time. He's going to be my protector. Lots of the younger kids have older kids watching out for them; not for money either, just somebody looking out. He already made me pass on one of the cars because he'd heard the guy's an asshole. When he finds out about the cheat guy, he adds him to that list.

It's good to have him looking out.

It's even better the next day, to walk into All American Boy and get the tight parachute pants I've tried on at least fifty times, and a crisp white button-up shirt. Tonight I'll make enough to get the black boots I've been wanting; the stacked heels make me taller.

*       *       *

Guys pull over — I'm making money. All of a sudden, life's good. I can choose things. I'm not begging or eating garbage. I can shop. I can have dinner at restaurants. I can get supplies from Longs Drugs. Sometimes I can even stay a night at a hotel. I'm taking care of myself.

I bleach my hair and gel it up. Once in a while I stay at this place on California around from The Masque or at the Royal Ambassador down by Market. You can only go where they don't really care; legitimate places won't rent to kids. Bathrooms are always down the hall. You got to be careful who sees you going in, and check out the hall before you go piss. Once I opened the door and this girl was getting beat up by her pimp. She wasn't even yelling or fighting back, just taking it. I think she was high on H. Another time, I got lice, which I didn't even know for a week. But it's okay most times; at least you're out of the weather.

I keep meeting other working kids and pretty soon I know tons. I fit in. We hustle together on Polk and hang out on Castro, proud that we can pay and not have to steal. It's important not to have a bad rep over there. Sometimes we get into clubs — the ones where we know the doorman, or our trick does. Except Nick, he never gets in. He looks even younger than me, like eleven or twelve.

"So? I get more dates," he says when I tease him. He does. Makes you wonder.

My whole life's at night now, from when people start cruising, as soon as it gets dark, until about four in the morning. The only part I hate is how tricks never look you in the eyes. How they seem to want to think it's your fault they're doing it.

I keep it fast and don't think too hard. One night I make almost three hundred dollars. Some nights, I may only get twenty. Or nothing. Sometimes the cops are out and you have to literally run and hide from them. Always, the "regular" people look disgusted when they see us. Even kids our own age. They roll their eyes or laugh or make faces. I keep hoping I'll get used to it, but I don't.

"Who cares about them?" Tommy says. "They don't know shit about anything, Jason. Where were they when your mom kicked you out?"

## {2}

Cruising down Polk toward us is a silver Corvette, low to the ground, sleek, awesome.

"Is that Jetsons, or what?" Adam points as the car makes the corner and heads down our block. He still thinks he's God's gift but he's so damn funny, I put up with it. The Corvette pulls to the curb in front of us. Adam pops up and smiles; the guy smiles back but beckons to me. He's older, maybe forty, and very distinguished looking, with a great moustache and amazing thick eyebrows.

"You look like you might enjoy Edith Piaf."

I have no idea what he's talking about.

"Of course I would," I say, folding my hands across my chest, looking at him through my lashes. The guys opens the door — it goes straight up! — and I climb in. This could be a sugar daddy, for sure. Adam flounces away.

His name is Barney. We go to a piano bar up on Nob Hill. I can't believe how classy it is. They all know him there, the maître d', the waiters, the guy at the piano. We sit at "his" table in the back near the stage, and I have my very first brandy. It makes my nose run. We eat hors d'oeuvres of shrimp and little pastries. A man who looks like a woman who looks like the painting my dad did of Judy Garland sings songs in French. Barney explains that Edith Piaf was a French torch singer and tells me about her life.

I can't stop staring at him as he talks — it's like watching a movie star. The word "elegant" comes to mind. I feel very grown-up and want to say all the right things but keep slipping and saying "yeah" instead of "yes" — and then giggling like I'm ten. Still, he asks me to spend the night and offers me $200. I tell him $300 and he winks.

"Smart boy," he says, then tousles my hair and agrees!

I've never stayed with anyone outside of the Castro, and definitely never for money. Barney lives way down on the Embarcadero, in a condo on a top floor where you can see the Bay and the city both. All white furniture with bright red and orange paintings on the walls, and squat African statues of men with big dicks and women with boobs. We have brandy on his balcony and he tells me about growing up in Chicago, about how he got into his career in film location scouting, then we go to bed.

I wake up alone; Barney's bustling about the kitchen. I love the feel of his sheets against my skin. The window curtains are drawn, patches of blue sky peek through the morning fog.

"Breakfast!" he calls. I slip on his shirt from the night before and find him the kitchen. He serves me an omelet with mushrooms and Swiss cheese. He is as elegant in his bathrobe as he was last night in a suit. We sit on the couch inside the French doors to eat and watch the fog drift daintily across the bay.

"Well, JJ, I like you. You're a sweet boy."

I smile like my face might break.

"I'm taking a few days off, going down to Carmel. I wonder if you'd like to come along?"

"Sure."

"Not for money, though. I can't afford three hundred a night. But I will show you a good time."

"Oh, that's fine. That's just fine." I float on air for the next hour. We pack up clothes for him, and stop by Macy's to pick up a few things for me. The car ride down is heaven. He plays Edith and I try to take in this incredible turn of events.

Barney's got a house on the beach. We shop for food and I love how he keeps me close, almost like I'm his son. We spend the next three days exploring the shore, cooking meals with food I've never even heard of, and being together. When he takes his binders and notebooks out to work, I sit quietly across from him, like I used to with my dad. The last night we're there, I creep out of bed sometime around three in the morning to sit on the balcony, wrapped up in Barney's pale yellow sweater. The rhythm of the surf could be my own heart. Each star shines brilliantly. I never realized there were so many. I never realized I could be so happy.

"Ah. Back to work." We're in Barney's apartment on our first morning after Carmel. "Would you like to drive up to the country with me?" he asks. "I'm scouting a location."

"Okay, yeah, sure," I say, taking my last bite of breakfast, wondering how much better it can get. I'm glad I didn't make up a totally different name; I'm looking for the best time to tell him JJ is short for Jason. We shower and dress and jump in the Corvette. He takes out part of the roof so I can look up and see the sky. Icy wind whips through my hair as we zoom across the Golden Gate Bridge. I stick my arms out and laugh. He plays jazz and smiles.

An hour up the 101, we exit. The roads get smaller as we head inland. Cows graze, and dilapidated old houses are scattered around. He finds the address he wants, parks the car near a barn and pokes around a bit. He takes several pictures with his Polaroid camera, makes notes, and climbs back inside. He tells me I'm good luck; he found exactly what he needed the first time out.

By the time we're coming back into the city, I'm trying to figure out how to best get in touch with Tommy to let him know about Barney. Maybe he can come visit. I suppose I'll be sleeping in Barney's room, but I'll be willing to go in the second bedroom too, when he needs his space. I'll keep him company on his scouting expeditions. I'll meet his friends, maybe even see a movie star or two when filming starts. I'd be cool with that. I can act right, not like some stupid little kid. Maybe I'll even get my break and be on TV.

Just off the bridge, Barney pulls into Clown Alley at the corner of Lombard and Divisadero.

"Let's get a little something to eat, shall we?" He buys us each a hot dog and we settle in at the little table on the side. He makes notes by the photos he's stuck in his binder while I count colors on cars, nibble at my hot dog, and wait to hear his words.

"So — JJ," he says, smiling. "You're a swell kid. I've had a really great time with you."

"Me too." I smile, bat my eyes at him, ready to tell him yes when he asks if I'll move in. He reaches for his wallet and I'm about to tell him don't worry about it.

"Can you get back from here?" he asks, and holds out three bills.

"Back?" My smile freezes. A stone drops into my gut.

"You know, to your — street? I have an appointment; I'm going to have to take off."

"Oh. Yes, of course, sure." I finally said "yes" instead of "yeah." Somehow I take the money and keep smiling, even though my face now feels heavy and dead. He pats my cheek and climbs back in his car. I finish my hot dog, wipe my mouth carefully, and toss the trash in the can. I've got to stop being so dumb. I wonder who will get to wear all my new clothes.

\*     \*     \*

Tommy catches up with me back in the Castro, grabs me by both shoulders, sticks his face close to mine. "Where the hell were you?"

I explain.

"You can't do that, Jason!" Adam jumps in. "You can't just leave with some guy because he's got a cool car. You gotta let somebody know where you're going. Shit happens. Tommy's been looking for you for days."

"I was fine," I say.

"You are so dumb," Tommy rants. You're going end up like Darren."

"Who's Darren?"

"A stupid kid like you. He went with some guy and didn't tell any-body. He got tied up in a warehouse on the Embarcadero. Three guys raped him, Jason. He managed to get back here and we took him to the hospital but —" Tommy has to stop.

"He died, Jason," Adam says. "He got all ripped up inside. He bled to death."

"Oh my God."

"Yeah," Tommy says.

"But it wasn't like that," I insist. "Barney bought me clothes. We went to Carmel, he cooked for me, he took me up with him to do his work —"

"*Barney* could just as easy have taken you into the park, done what he wanted, and dumped you."

"But he didn't," I say, as a chill surrounds my spine, creeps through the rest of my body. I think where we were today, down a road with no houses near; I remember the isolation of the cottage in Carmel. No-body would have found me in either place, or known who I was if they did. Working boys don't carry I.D.'s.

"Please don't be stupid anymore, okay?" Tommy says. "You tell us. Let somebody know."


I can't help myself. I call the number Barney gave me, but it isn't even his. The days get longer and tourists pour in, so there's new tricks, but also more kids getting hurt. Nick gets a black eye from an asshole who then rapes him. Now, every time a car pulls up, I make a plan — what I'll do if something happens. I keep a hand on the door handle and constantly check to make sure they don't hit automatic lock. Sometimes, if the guy looks creepy, I open the window so I can crawl through if I need to.

One day becomes the next and it's hard to keep track; I'm tired all the time. More and more straight people come down to Polk Street to stare at us and act shocked, or laugh. I hate them. How they think *we're* the freaks. I start to worry I'll end up here, that I'll never meet somebody and just fall in love. I want to stop, but I can't go back to eating garbage.

## {3}

"Let's go."

Tommy raps on the bathroom door. We're at the Shell station, me, Nick, Adam, Miles, and Dan, all finishing up our hair, crowding in to see the mirror. Tommy's arranged a date. There's a limo waiting. The guy's a doctor. He lives in one of those huge mansions out in the rich section on Broadway. The car lets us out in the back alley and we go through what's obviously the service entrance.

"Tommy?" I ask, "are you sure about this?"

"Shh. Yes. Stop complaining."

I'm not complaining, but I don't much like how he's been acting recently — like he's tough shit and in charge of everyone. But how do I say no? He's taken care of me all this time. I shrug and follow Nick into the house. We hang out in a huge living room while Tommy goes up the stairs. An ordinary-looking guy with glasses and a balding head comes back down with him, smiling at all of us. He's tall and reminds me of my uncle.

"Hello, boys," he says. "Welcome to my house." Another man appears, holding a doctors' tray, the kind that usually has instruments to look up your nose. This one has syringes.

"What the hell's this?" Adam says.

"What's going on?" Nick asks.

"Don't worry about it," Tommy says. "You'll like it." I've never seen him so pushy; I feel like I'm hanging out with Davy. The doctor's friend picks up a syringe and looks over at us, smiling.

"I'll go," says Dan, and we all watch as the guy ties off his arm, like a nurse does — or a junkie — and injects a vein in his arm.

"Now, that didn't hurt, did it?"

Dan smiles, says "whoo" and plops down on the couch. I go next. He's right, the needle's not painful — but the second it's done, I get a ringing in my ears and my heart starts to race. Then I have to puke, but the doctor's ready for this and has a pan right there. What he's given me is a speedball. I don't know this until later, much later. It's cocaine and heroin mixed together. You throw up from the heroin, but after, you feel amazing, or at least I did — mellow but with energy and horny as hell. I laugh. I can't seem to stop laughing.

More people come, people we don't know, but I don't care too much. I dance with Nick. I dance with some short gray-haired man. Some-body plays Donna Summer, then the Village People — over and over again. Nick takes his clothes off, which seems like a great idea, so I do too. Pretty soon we're all naked. I don't see Tommy anywhere. Things happen in flashes but it all seems okay. I'm still laughing. We go to an-other room and the doctor takes pictures. Now it's real flashes. This makes me laugh too. I think I must be a big boy, finally, because I can have my picture taken naked and it's not at all scary. Tommy comes out of nowhere and takes my hand and leads me somewhere with some-one — I don't remember who. I smell something sweet, maybe a candle burning? We take more drugs, I'm not even sure what.

Then it's morning and I'm standing naked on a balcony by myself. I'm sore everywhere. I don't know what time it is, what day it is even. I don't know how long we've been here. I find Adam curled up asleep on a couch in a downstairs living room. At first he won't wake up and I freak. What did we do? Where is everybody? Why did Tommy bring us here? Adam moans and turns over.

The doctor appears in the doorway. He doesn't look friendly now; he's not smiling. He's all business. "Okay, boys. Time to get dressed and go on home. The car's waiting."

"Where's our money?" Nick asks.

"You've been paid. Now, please go."

"Where's Tommy?" I ask.

"Waiting for you in the car. Now go."

On the ride back, Tommy gives us each a hundred dollar bill.

"That's it?" Adam says. Tommy doesn't answer. He's in the front with the driver. He won't even look me in the eyes. The car drops him off first, at Market, near Van Ness; he marches down the street without saying a word. The rest of us are let out down by Castro. I'm embarrassed. I don't know why. I head off too, and end up slipping into the nook where I used to stay. Something important has changed, and I don't even know what it is.

Tommy and me never talk about it again, none of us do — we all act like nothing happened.

A couple weeks after that, I catch one of those really awful summer colds, probably from the shitty hotels I've been staying in. It goes down into my chest; I cough constantly. My voice gets low and raspy.

"I think it's sexy," says the trick who's buying me drinks that night. We're in The Masque and I'm feeling worse by the minute. I wish Tommy was around, but he's not really watching out for me anymore. I remember my dad once saying that drinking alcohol is good when you're sick — it kills the bacteria. So I figure if I have a few drinks, then go to sleep after this guy, I'll be fine in the morning. Except my head starts to throb so bad I can barely see straight. I tell the guy I'll see him later.

"Why don't you try this?" says the trick. He digs into his pocket and brings out a prescription bottle, shakes out two tablets. "It's my sinus medication," he tells me. "Fix you right up."

I take a good long look at him. He reminds me of that movie where Don Knotts turns into a fish.

"Thanks anyway," I say, "but I think I better just go on home."

"All right." He sounds disappointed but puts the tablets away. "At least let me pay for your cab."

For some reason, I think this means he's a great guy, that all he wants is for me to be okay — and I change my mind. I swallow the tablets with my drink. It's the last thing I remember.

I wake up outside an apartment building with no idea where I am or how long I've been there. My head aches. I'm still snotty. I don't know if it's the next day or the next week. I don't know what I've done or what's been done to me. I stand up. I'm in my same clothes and even have the fifty that had been in my back pocket. I wasn't robbed. I don't hurt; I wasn't raped. The sun's in the middle of the sky, so it must be around noon.

The Transamerica Building peeks up over the others so I'm still in San Francisco. But this is definitely not okay. I don't know where I've been or what I've done. This is not okay. I can't keep putting myself in situations where I can get hurt. I have to figure out how to take control of my life. Nobody else is going to do that for me.

## {4}

"Well. I'm off to L.A.," Jimmy V announces. Jimmy V's older, twenty maybe. We think he deals. He's in and out of the city, and sometimes he hangs out with us when he's here. He always has stuff to share. When I'm not working, I appreciate it.

"Right now?" I ask. "Can I go?"

"Sure, why not?"

"Let me get my stuff." I grab my backpack and duck behind to where I keep my other clothes. Tommy glares at me.

"Are you serious?" Tommy says.

"I think so."

"You're just gonna leave?"

"Yeah. Tommy, it's L.A.! It's my chance. I'm gonna be an actor, remember?"

"Fine. Bye. Have a great life," he says, getting up.

"Why don't you come with me? You and me, we can —"

"I hate L.A.," he says and walks away.

"Tommy!" I run after him, grab his arm, swing him around. "Come on, don't be a bitch!"

"You're the one leaving."

"Why shouldn't I? What do I have here?" I blurt. His face clouds. "Besides you, I mean." He starts off again. "Tommy! Just come with me."

He turns. "I can't be in L.A., Jason. Too much happened there, I just . . . I can't."

"Yeah? Well, same with me, here." As I say it, I know it's true.

He stares and I watch his eyes close down. "Fine. Do what you want. I sure as hell don't care."

This time he doesn't stop. Calling after him doesn't help; he holds up his middle finger. For a second, I want to follow and apologize and stay — but you know what? Friendship goes both ways. Besides, it's my life, I need to be in charge of it. Los Angeles is where movies get made, and people get rich. San Francisco gets cold. L.A. does not. I grab my last pack of cigarettes and jam the rest of my stuff into my backpack. I tuck a twenty and two tens in my pocket and follow Jimmy V to his gold Dodge Charger.

*     *     *

We smoke our cigarettes, listen to KFRC, and head over the Bay
Bridge to the 580, to catch the I-5 going south. As we veer right onto
the interstate, I suddenly realize that no one in my family will know
where I am. I feel a tug on my heart.

I see myself in the garage at the old house, sitting on my dad's big
bike, watching him paint, feeling safe. Then I hear him say: *"It's between you and your mother now."* I see myself in class with Davy, then
with him in the hallway, when he told me just to go. I see Marianne,
painting her nails, always taking care of me. I sigh. My mother laughing, looking beautiful in her yellow dress. Closing the front door. Turning out the lights. Calling me that name. The feeling now is more than
sadness. I'm just hollow, there's nothing there.

We take the ramp to the I-5.

"Got any more of that weed?" I ask.

We pull off at Highland and stop for a light before turning onto Hollywood Boulevard. The streets sparkle for real here — glistening bits of
stuff in the concrete, with famous people's names in stars all down the
sidewalks. I lean out the window by Mann's Chinese and try to make
out one or two.

"Jimmy, look," I say, "there's Marilyn Monroe's hand prints! There's
Judy Garland!"

He chuckles as I sit back, grinning. Every kind of person imaginable
is out on this street. Lights and billboards and energy everywhere; in
comparison, Castro's boring and Polk Street doesn't even make the
chart. We turn down La Brea to Santa Monica Boulevard — which I've
heard about — and go west. He pulls over for cigarettes at a liquor
store by a street called Curson. I think it's funny: Curse On.

"Kools for me," Jimmy V says, and holds out a dollar. He points at
the "no stopping" sign. "I'll make the block."

"My treat," I say as I hop out the car. The woman behind the counter watches me like a hawk, but doesn't ask for I.D. I get his Kools and a pack of Marlboros for me, and go outside to wait.

I light up, check around. Just down the street is a place called Oki Dogs and realize I'm starving. Maybe we can grab a bite before we head to his friend's place. I check around the corner and up and down the street. What the hell's taking so long?

"You looking for the guy in the gold car?" This from the cute, curly-haired kid on the bus bench nearby.

"Yeah."

"He split, man. Soon as you got out."

I freeze, blink. "You sure?"

"Didn't wait a second."

Everything I own is in the back of his car. Why would he do this? How can I still be so dumb?

"What do I do now?" I say out loud, not meaning to.

"How should I know?" He hops down, stomps off.

It's late, the air's turning moist, and though it's not nearly as cold as the city, I picture my jacket hanging over the front seat. I take a breath and get my thoughts together. I may not know L.A., but men in cars? A gay boy on the bench? Cops around and gay bars down both sides of the street? That park we passed will have kids sleeping in it. I decide against fast food. I go back to the liquor store to try to exchange the Kools.

"Sure, why not?" the woman says, not looking so mean this time. I grab cookies and milk to eat when I find a place to stay, and as I take them up to the counter, glance at the show biz magazines sitting in the rack alongside.

"Anniversary of the Death of the King!"

"Elvis Gone Two Years Today!"

Well hell. It's my birthday. Might as well get some chips too. I just turned fourteen years old.

# 1979

Fear, China White, and T.S.O.L. are at the Starwood and the club's packed. Not a severely hardcore crowd, except for the Orange County LADS that show up. And me.

Punk's changing again, evolving. I'm moving with it.

I definitely lean toward hardcore. Can't stand the New Wave shit and I hate people who get involved with Punk just for the look of it. Stupid jocks, preppies cutting their hair, thinking they're cool now. They're into the fashion of it. Fashion is bullshit. They're showing up everywhere. Getting into the circle. Pissing me off. Even skanking's not doing it for me anymore. It's cheap, just another thing. I'm looking for something more.

Punk is a way of life. Not a weekend diversion.

"Like your tattoo," the skinhead bouncer says. He's older, huge, definitely will not take shit from anyone. Lots of skinheads work the Punk scene. He nods at the newest one on my arm—a death's head with a snake curving through the eye sockets.

"Thanks." I check his arms — he's got WHITE POWER in fancy letters, and a huge swastika over the American flag. He sees me looking, flexes his arm, and the flag ripples.

"Just stating my cause, my friend."

"Yeah." I'm not sure what he means but I'm not about to argue.

"This country belongs to the white people. Remember that." He checks a group that's just come into the club, then turns back to me. "We got to look out for each other, my friend. Make sure we get the respect we deserve. Otherwise the whole country's going down." He winks and turns to yell at a kid trying to crash the door.

Fear is outstanding.

In between sets, there's some kind of commotion on the stairs. People are screaming at each other, throwing chairs and anything they can lift. We go to check it out. The Orange County LADS are somehow in the mix, I see them converging. Suddenly one of the bouncers comes tumbling down the staircase. It's like watching a stuntman. Everybody gets out of the way. He lands hard on the floor; people press around him.

"Man, his guts are falling out," Jack says.

"Is he dead?" Stacie asks.

"I don't know," I say. "I don't want to know."

It's not the skinhead I talked with earlier. *He's* trying to get people to make some room around the guy who fell.

"Let's book it," I say, but by the time we find everybody, the cops have shut down the place, locked the doors. There's no way out. It gets intense quick. Everybody watches everybody else. Nobody knows what happened, who did it. I'm thinking the LADS. Paramedics put the bouncer on a stretcher. His eyes are open but he's not moving.

The cops herd the young scared wannabes to the stage area. Hardcore gets pushed to the back hall. They separate girls and guys and start to frisk us all. A Mexican cop shoves my nose into the concrete wall, twists my arm behind me so hard it makes my eyes water. "Freak," he mutters, and his black buddy pats me down, shoving his hand so hard up against my balls my knees go weak. I don't hold the knife anymore, I learned that at Jenna's party. All my stuff's in the car, except the box cutter I carry now, which I managed to lose before the cops got to me. I don't say anything. I think on the skinhead's words.

"This nightclub will be closed from now on," says a voice over the loudspeaker. What he means is there won't be any more *Punk* here. Two of the LADS are handcuffed and shoved into the police van. The rest of us get in our cars. It's like this all over now. We don't do a thing and still get pushed around, stopped on the street for nothing.

"Don't you dare speed," Rosie warns, as Stacie pulls out. Me and Jack are in the back. We don't even play music on the way to Oki Dogs. We sit staring straight ahead, getting pissed. We pass a couple of hippies walking down Highland. Usually, that'd be an invitation to jump out and kick ass. Tonight we don't bother. Stacie parks at Astro Burger and we head across the street.

Even Oki Dog's not the same. It used to be Punks from all over L.A., the Inland Empire, Orange County even, would meet up here late at night and hang out. Nobody else'd dare come by, not if they didn't want to get hassled. Now there's all kinds of people, all the time. Nobody gives a damn about us.

Stace and them hang out front smoking cigarettes. I get in line, thinking on respect, fighting for what belongs to you.

"You want buy some shit?" the chink behind the counter asks the woman in front of me. "What kind shit you want?"

I look up and notice she's got a great ass, and dressed to show it off. Maybe my night just got better. I check to make sure Stacie's not looking and cup her cheek with one hand.

"Hey!" she says in a husky low voice, "you can look, honey, but you can't touch unless you got some cash."

She turns around and my mouth drops — *she's a HE*.

"Sick faggot bastard," I say, hoping no one saw. He doesn't flinch.

"Yeah, whatever, baby," he says. "You the one rubbing." He winks, flicks his tongue out, grabs his Oki Dog, and swishes his way out the door.

"What kind shit for you?" the counter guy asks. I don't know how I manage to get the food, pay, and join up with Stacie and them outside. How I manage to eat, or carry on any kind of conversation. I'm done with this day. Too much input. The jet plane's revving up in my head.

"Let's go," I say and start for the car.

"I'm still eating," Stacie says. I don't stop. Stacie cusses but follows. I sit in the back and listen to Rosie, Jack, and her chatter away. I have nothing to say. Every stupid thing I never want to think about is popping up in my head, wanting attention. My father staring from the doorway as I lay there in the body cast; Carl, getting shot, getting beat; the skinhead I talked to earlier.

I'm doing nothing with my life. Going nowhere. Even my music sucks. It's all chaos now, everything. Inside me and in this whole damn world. From me living half at Stacie's and half at home, to faggots taking over at Oki Dogs, to this noise inside my brain. I am losing my control. My mind spins in loops and I don't know how to stop it. I got no landing place, no safety anywhere. I feel like running my head into a wall. There is simply no way out.

# 1979

### FIVE MONTHS BEFORE

### LOS ANGELES COUNTY

"Coco LaMere is *not* your real name." I poke him in the ribs as I say it. I tease him relentlessly these days. We've been hanging out for a while. He's the kid I first saw on the bench.

"Bitch, please, you don't know me," he tosses back, takes a huge bite of his second Astro Burger, everything on it. Where he puts it all, I don't know, he's the skinniest boy I've ever seen. And the cutest, with that dark curly hair and exotic face. I like him, more than just a little.

"This name goes back generations." He says it with his mouth full.

"Uh-huh, and your mama's working Sunset."

"At least she can get work. More than I can say for your ugly mama." Car doors slam and we both turn to see a carload of skinheads piling out of an old station wagon.

"Oh well," Coco says, rolling his eyes. "There goes the neighborhood."

"Don't worry. They're going to Oki Dogs," I say.

"Oh, too bad. The tall one's sexy," Coco says.

"If you like Neo-Nazis."

"I like the tattoos."

"You would."

"Do you think they do it on their dicks?"

"Ew. Ow."

*       *       *

"Check that out," Coco says, and nods toward the shadow of a guy peeking out at us from inside a chocolate-colored Bentley. We're lounging on my bench, across from where Jimmy dropped me off. I chose it to remind myself not to be a dumbass.

"No way," I say. "He wants you." The guy honks lightly.

"I don't think so, sweetie. Definitely a J-man." Coco gives a little push. I look again. Why not? It's early, I'm not too tired. Besides, you never know. This might be the sugar daddy I'm always looking for. He drives a Bentley, doesn't he?

I ease off the bench, adjust my pants, touch my hair.

"You're so effin' sexy," Coco says and winks. I smile down at him, feeling that little tingle. We look good together. He squeezes my hand and whispers, "So, later? Want to hang out? You'll be rich then, you can buy us dinner."

I nod and wish the Bentley guy wasn't there so I could give him a little kiss. "Wish me luck, babe," I say and step into the street, lean into the Bentley. Still thinking about Coco, I put my head down and peek up through my lashes. The guy smiles at me.

"Pretty eyes," he says. He's older, maybe fifty, sixty.

"Thanks."

"Shall we?"

"For sure."

He reaches to open the door. "Come on in."

I do. He's skinny — thank God, I won't go with fat guys. We turn up Curse-On and he finds a place to pull over.

"How much?" he asks.

"Thirty, I'll use my hand. Fifty, you get both."

"Both, and a twenty-dollar tip if I can see you naked."

I consider it. As a rule, I never get completely undressed, but dinner would be amazing and I do know how to roll my pants down so I can run, if I have to. Besides, I could skip work for the night and spend the time with Coco.

"All right," I say, "but you can't finish while I'm there. Okay?"

"Okay."

"I mean that."

"Fine."

He takes way longer than I expect. I check around to see where his wallet is, if maybe I can snatch it and run. In that one second, when I'm off guard, he grabs my head and holds it down. I fight back, hitting at him and trying to bite. I scratch the inside of his thigh, everything — but it's too late. He yanks me up by my hair, then slaps me. His face is red and he's breathing hard. I hold out one hand and try to get my pants up with the other. He gives me a bill.

"That's only twenty!"

"Get out of my car."

"Where's my money, fuckface, you said okay!"

Without any warning, he shoves, hard, and I tumble out the door, onto my hands and knees, bare butt in the air. He laughs. I whip around and catch his eyes; this enrages him. I have to duck as the door slams back, just missing my head. The asshole drives away, going home to a wife, I know this — I saw the ring. Maybe even kids. I wonder if he has boys. If one of them's fourteen.

For the briefest second, I remember Paul crying, my uncle's mouth tightening, my surprise when that very first trick couldn't look at me. I

scoot up onto the sidewalk, pull up my pants, look around, take inven-
tory. At least nobody saw. But shit, the knee's torn on my jeans and
there's blood on my white shirt. I can't see Coco like this.

*What is Davy doing right now?* I wonder.

*I should've paid attention.*

*Where's Marianne? Would she hate me if she knew?*

*Do any of them even miss me?*

I shake my head, stand up. I need to take care of myself now and
stop thinking stupid thoughts.

I see the kid as I cross the street back to the park to get a change of
clothes. He's so scared and fresh I can't look at him.

"Excuse me?" he whispers, as I pass. "Could you —" He sees my
torn clothes and bloody arms and gasps.

"What?" I ask, not nicely. He's a rich little kid, I can tell right off —
expensive clothes, *great* haircut. He immediately bursts into tears,
putting his hands up to hide his face. I want to walk past him, but think
of Tommy helping me the night after my mother and the cop. If I don't
stop, I'm my father who turned away, my brother who didn't want me,
my mother who slapped my face.

"Okay. What's your name?" I demand.

"Tim. Timmy." He's soft like a puppy.

"How old are you?" I say.

"Almost twelve."

"Go home," I say.

"I can't." He cries again.

I see it in his eyes. He's right, whatever happened to him there, he
can't go back. "At least go wash your face, okay? You got snot all over."
I point down the street toward Highland. "Shell station, on the corner.
Ask for the key, pretend your dad's in the car. You got money?"

He pulls out a fistful of twenties. I slap his hand back.

"Don't do that. Don't show people your money." I shake my head. "You gotta wise up, little dude, or you'll be dead by morning."

"Okay, okay, I will." He looks at me like I'm God or something.

"Buy some food, hear? Then find a place in the park you can sleep. Make sure nobody can sneak up on you. Don't talk to anybody, okay? Look me up tomorrow."

"Okay." He almost smiles. "Thank you." He leans in like I'm going to hug him or something but I turn away. I'm dirty and pissed off and my favorite shirt is torn and now I've got to get ready to go to work.

# 1980

I don't know what it is about Punk at our school now; suddenly it's cool and everywhere and Evelyn Anderson wants to hang out. She sidles up to me at lunch. She lets me cop a feel in the field at lunch. She even follows me out after school when Stace comes to pick me up.

"A Barbie, Doug?" Rosie says, the next day. "Give me a break. What's the hell's wrong with you?"

"You see those tits?" I snap back.

"You'll be sorry, dude," she says. I don't think so. I think it's fine if I hang out with a Barbie at school. Stacie has her own friends. Besides, I'm back at home now, most of the time. Either that or my parents will make me move out completely, which is not possible until I can finish school and get a job.

Saturday, Stace and Rosie and I head down to Wong's East to see a new band we've been hearing about. Apparently, everybody else in L.A. has heard about them too — the place is packed, and the line goes down the street. Carlos appears right behind us, just before we get to the door. Carlos is the old boyfriend, slick and Latin and all Punked out. He slips his arm around Rosie and she likes it.

"Did you know he'd be here?" I ask Stacie as we go in.

"Got a problem with that?"

"Hell, I don't care what you do."

"Good." She leaves me and goes right over to talk to him and Rosie. They're all laughing together and rubbing up against each other and I head out back to snort some shit with some guy I meet. I don't even know what it is. I score a bottle from the same guy. I drink and rub up on girls and then go to skank. Stacie doesn't seem to notice. Rosie's having a great time. Everybody is, it seems, but me. The band's not even that good. Whatever it is I snorted kicks off a major headache. I look for a way to get home, but can't find anybody that goes my way. I have to go with Stacie.

I finally locate her outside in the back alley, with a whole group of chicks her own age, Rosie, and the Latin asshole.

"Come on. I wanna split."

"Then split," Stacie says. "What's stopping you?"

Carlos claps me on the shoulder. "Patience, *mi amigo*," he says, like we know each other. "Let the ladies finish talking."

I want to hit him. But my skull feels like it's cracking open so I just go lean against the wall until Stacie walks by and beckons me to follow. We pile in her car, Carlos and Rosie in the backseat. I put in the Dead Kennedys and try to forget the headache, but by the time we drop Rosie off, I'm in serious pain.

"Denny's?" Rosie asks.

"Good idea, I'm starved," says Carlos.

"Drop me at home, okay?" I don't even care anymore if she wants to hang out with him.

"Why? You meeting your little cheerleader?" Stacie says and Carlos laughs. She glances back. "He thinks I don't know."

My head's bursting. "Shut up, you don't know shit."

She pulls over to the side of the road. "Why don't you just get out, huh? Go see Barbie. I'm tired of playing with kids."

"Stace—"

"Get out of my car."

"Fine. Whatever." I get out and go to slam the door, but Carlos catches it and slips inside the front. I hear them laughing as she drives away. I stand alone in the middle of the street. I'm seven blocks from my parents' home. The neighborhood is completely still. I start to walk.

This whole stupid world's pissing me off.

I kick at a mailbox, one of those ones on wood posts, with a metal top. It hurts my foot, which makes me kick it again. It takes a couple of hard blows, but then it breaks, right in two, and clangs down on the concrete. The black iron dog on top snaps off. A light goes on in the house across the street. A door opens next door and a man's voice cries out, *"What's going on out there?"*

I run at the next box and kick it until it falls. The one after is free-standing chain, and I miss, fall, hurt my hip on the curb. I cuss, as loud as I can. More doors are opening, more porch lights turning on. I take off down the street.

I feel better already.

Sirens sound. More lights flick on. Now I want somebody to go get my parents. I want my mother and father to see what I'm doing. I want them to know who their son really is. I want my dad to try and stop me.

The damage you do has to feel right.

You got to stand up for yourself.

You can't let fucking faggot whores take over what belongs to you.

You have to fight for what you believe.

My rampage takes me down one street and up to the next, a cul-de-sac. The sirens get louder. Two cop cars pull up on either side of the corner yard where I now stand. Four cops pile out—three guys and a chick, guns drawn and pointed directly at me.

"Shoot me!" I yell, holding my hands up in the air. "Shoot me, motherfucker!"

People peek from their porches, peer through windows. Nobody knows what to do with me, not even the cops.

"Go ahead, shoot me!!"

"Get your hands up!"

"Down on the ground!"

They smell like the slam pit as they circle around, all of them yelling. The noise of them seeps in my head.

"Get down! Get down! Get down!" The cop that's talking edges closer. His eyes dart back and forth and I wonder if he'll shoot me. I think he probably will. I start to laugh and his eyes go dark. Suddenly I think of Rosie. What would happen to her, without me here to protect her? This is big. This needs consideration. I put my hands behind my head, legs out.

Two other cops rush me, knock me facedown and drag my arms back behind me. They haul me over and the next thing I know I'm on the sidewalk on my knees, hands in cuffs behind me. Something gets tied around the cuffs and one of the cops pulls it straight up so I'm bowing forward. My head almost touches the ground. My hip has gone on fire.

"Jeez, Mike, he's just a kid," the woman cop says. She puts her gun back in its holster, buckles it in. She's not much bigger than Stacie, with dark hair pulled straight back.

"I don't care, he's on something. Keep back."

She doesn't. She comes in close, kneels down, and looks dead in my eyes. "What's going on, dude?" she asks. "What is it?"

I give her my hardest glare but she doesn't flinch. She looks up behind me. "Will you please loosen that up?"

"It could be PCP, Jo."

"Yeah, and what's he going to do? Huh? He can't move and if he does, you got a gun pointing at his head." She sits down beside me.

"What's your name?"

"Fuck you."

"Nice talk. I'm Jo Ann. What's your name?" She touches the side of my face, brushing something away. I jerk my head away from her and the cop yanks my arms.

"Stop it, Mike!" she says. She takes my chin in her hand. I flinch at her touch. She doesn't let go. "Tell me your name, dude."

"Doug."

"Good. Thanks. What's wrong, Doug? What happened?"

"Why should I tell you anything?"

"Because I'm asking."

"Why the fuck do you care?"

"I don't know. You're a kid. I like kids. How old are you, Doug?"

"Nineteen."

"No you're not."

I don't know why I tell her the truth. "Sixteen. Almost seventeen." She adjusts herself to block the other cops from being able to see my face. I focus on her eyes. She's got nice eyes. Hazel brown.

"Sixteen's a hard age to be."

"No shit."

"Tonight was pretty bad?"

"Every fucking night is bad."

"But tonight, something worse?"

"It was shit," I mutter. "A real fucking bad night."

I can't believe I'm talking to her. I try to adjust my body so my hip won't hurt so much. I get my arms yanked.

"Watch out, Jo Ann!"

"Relax, would you?" Jo Ann calls back. She reaches behind and makes them let up. She has a sad smile on. "Girlfriend?"

"Yeah." I tell her about Stacie and how my music's not working for me anymore, how the bouncer last week got stabbed and the cops slammed me up against the wall, how my hip has a metal pin. Everything. It pours out. Like I have no control. She doesn't interrupt. She invites me to sit down with her and makes the other cops help me do it. They keep their guns pointed at my head. She makes them take me home.

My mother cries with that stupid whimper sound of hers. My father stares into space. You'd think he'd go off, but he never does, not with cops. He's not so tough with authority.

Jo Ann explains that I won't be arrested, but a bill will be sent for damaged property. She tells my parents I need to get counseling, something to help me deal with stuff. My mother nods. My father gets up and walks out of the room. Jo Ann leaves and my mother fixes me something to eat. I can't eat it. I can't do anything. My hip hurts like crazy. I wonder if there are any painkillers in the house. Anything.

# 1980

TWO MONTHS BEFORE

LOS ANGELES COUNTY

"See what I mean?" Coco says. "L.A. Sunny Southern. You can't beat it."

He's right. We're on the boardwalk down at Venice Beach, walking around in T-shirts when Tommy's probably huddling under a bench somewhere. The sun shines down on a whole universe of people — every kind imaginable. A black guy in a Jesus robe and harem pants roller-skates past, a boombox on his shoulder, singing along. His hair's down to his waist, wound into dreds. People sit along the sidewalk on blankets, selling jewelry and T-shirts and pretty much anything you could think of. All kinds of music, all types of accents, all shades of skin. An old woman with no front teeth offers to read our Tarot cards.

"Not so bad, babe, huh?" Coco asks, slipping an arm over my shoulders.

"I like it."

"See? Sometimes you got to check things out, you know? There's a whole world out there we don't even know about."

We get to Venice Boulevard, where the boardwalk loops onto the street, and turn back. I feel like a little kid. I can't believe I was scared about coming here. We get pizza from a stand and go watch a whole group of buffed-out guys lifting weights.

"Muscle beach," Coco explains. "Check out the guy in the blue."

"Amazing."

We take off our shoes and head down to the ocean. Coco shows me how to dig out a seat for myself. Under the top layer, the sand is cool and moist. We take off our shirts and settle in. Coco reaches for my hand. At first I look around, but it's okay. There are couples everywhere.

I find myself getting sleepy in the sun, lulled by the sound of the waves. When I look up again, he's staring at me, a sweet smile on his face.

"What?" I ask, smiling back.

"You. Your eyes. Your craziness. Everything. I just love you."

"I love you too."

## ONE MONTH BEFORE
## LOS ANGELES

"Take that fucking shirt off right now," I say. "Who do you think you are coming here with that stupid shirt?"

Rules have changed. Again.

The skinhead thing is getting intense. Lines are blurred.

Hardcore does not put up with shit like we used to. Like this guy up in my face right now, this stupid couple in their matching KISS shirts. Who the hell do they think they are? This is not the place for that shit. We're at the Olympic Auditorium; we got Punks here from L.A., Orange County, the Inland Empire. There are some violent groups and they're thinking the same thing as me but they don't have the balls to say it.

I do. I'm not in the mood.

"I said, take it off."

"Shut up, you creep," the girl says, sticking up for her boyfriend.

"You shut up!" he says to her. He doesn't utter a word to me. He knows what's around. He knows he fucked up.

"Take that stupid shit off," I say, and he does. They try to blend back into the crowd, but I see some of the Punk girls closing in and they get the girl's shirt too. That's the way it should be. The couple disappears.

Later, in the slam pit, I'm feeling pretty good until something sharp stabs into my side. I turn to see the KISS asshole grinning. The motherfucker came back and stabbed me! He's got one of those big safety pins that chefs use to hold their aprons together, sharpened. He snuck back in and fucking stabbed me in the ribs.

He takes off. I chase him up through the bleachers and then down into the walkway, which is where I beat the fuck out of him. I grab him by the hair and smash his face against the concrete steps. Bouncers pull me off, big black guys with yellow SECURITY shirts. I know I'm about to get a beating, so I show them the blood on my palm and then my side where the asshole cut me.

"Not even face-to-face," I tell them. "He stabbed me from the back, man, I didn't even see it coming."

"That's wrong, dude," the bigger guy says. "That's just wrong." They let me go. Later I hear they took the guy outside and kicked his ass.

All I want to do now is beat people up. Or get beat up myself. I don't particularly care which. I look for it. Like when I'm in the slam pit at the Warehouse and this big guy is standing there, this wannabe skinhead, not doing shit to me or anybody, just standing. But he's taller than me and that's enough. I know he's thinking he's tough shit. That he's like some Greek Fucking God. I hit him. He's surprised, so I hit him again.

I can't seem to get enough. When I'm not doing it, I'm thinking about it. I like how it feels. Every time, I know how bad it's gonna get, how fucking much it's gonna hurt. Every time, I get terribly afraid. My whole body shakes, my knees quiver, my blood turns cold. But I don't run. I don't move out of the way. I sure as shit don't hide. I move *into* the pain. I meet it head-on. That roar in my brain starts revving up, pushes me forward. It's like the best music I ever wrote.

Next comes the excitement, the challenge, putting myself to the test once again. What will happen? Will the victim fight? Will he try to run away? I don't mind chasing somebody. I usually catch them. When the victim fights back, that's the best. That's when you really have your work cut out for you.

Getting hit the first time *always* hurts, hurts like hell—electricity shooting through from wherever is the point of impact, up to the brain where it explodes again. That's the trigger, that's where the change occurs. They hit me again, but now I don't feel it. Now I'm numb to it, and time does that delicious slow motion thing, and I'm moving forward again—getting hit more and more, hitting back and feeling how that is, my fist on their flesh, always forward. It's awesome.

Like inhaling and expanding, I swell up. I get *huge*. Strong. God-like. It doesn't matter who or what or why—victims are totally inter-changeable, and always disposable. Sometimes they don't really even register. They're not people, they're not important. What's important is the release of action—the stretch of sinews, the flex of muscles, that incredible rush of adrenaline, filling me up and pushing me out-wards—at the same time, protecting me and spurring me on.

My war.

My tribe.

All my people feel the same.

Rosie, Jack, people we don't even know yet. We beat up hippies, jocks, stoners, other Punks. Anyone who looks at us funny. The police. It doesn't matter. They're all the same. They're not people, not when we're doing it. Most of the time, we got nothing against them personally.

We just need it.

It's part of life. So we do it.

Violence is now my best drug.

I won't lie.

I am a total addict.

# March 27, 1980

THE DAY OF

LOS ANGELES COUNTY

I'm awake but not here yet, not quite. I reach for my Listerine and rinse out, spit over against the wall, then yawn. Sun's up, full and bright. My eyes feel like sand's been poured in; my head throbs.

It's got to be past noon, but probably not by much. My elbow aches and my right hand burns pins and needles — I slept on it. I rub it and stretch, notice a little tribe of ants around a dead grasshopper. I yawn and watch for a while; they demolish the body piece by piece and haul it back to their little hill. They march in two straight lines, one coming, one going. I put a pebble in the way; they don't miss a step, just circle around it and keep on.

Go, ants.

A phone rings from one of the apartments next door. "*Hola*?" says a woman's voice. She chuckles deep in her throat and launches into gossip — all in Spanish but I can still tell. The guy from one building over lugs a smelly brown garbage bag down the alley. He doesn't see me through the fence; I'm tucked into the corner, out of his direct line of sight. He picks his nose and eats it — he always does, and I always gag, and then he empties his garbage.

This time of day, the park sucks. Too many people, too many eyes, nothing to do. I roll my shoulders and move my head from side to side, reach into my back pocket to see what's left from last night. I smile, remembering how funny Coco was. He was high on Tina and kept me laughing the entire night. It's working out with us, I know it. Even though we don't actually talk about it, I think probably we'll try to find a place soon, especially if we can find some older guys to go in on it. Yawning, I stretch both arms out and check around to see who's up. I wonder if I should wash first or head down to McDonald's. I'm not that hungry so maybe washing's good. The Listerine didn't help — I don't like the taste in my mouth.

Then I see her — a black-haired woman walking across the basketball court straight toward me. She has her hand up to her forehead to shield her eyes from the sun, so I can't see her face. I don't have to. I know the walk. I catch the energy, like a jolt of electricity. I even recognize the blouse.

It's my mother. She's found me.

Should I run? I'm already reaching back for my stuff, I could pack up in a sec and be out around the corner, go find Coco, hide out until —

NO.

That's not how she's walking. She's not angry, she's looking. She's smiling! What's going on? Why is she here? Could it be she changed her mind?

*That's stupid.*

*Is it?*

*Why would I care?*

*Because she's my mother and I love her.*

*Grow up.*

*I can't help it.*

Without taking my eyes off her, I reach for my mirror, digging down inside my backpack where I keep it wrapped in paper towels from the gas station. Quick check — I'm a mess! My hair sticks out on one side, and lies flat on the other; it's stiff from too much gel, a day past washing. There's a smudge on my forehead and waffle marks on one cheek from sleeping against my backpack. Shit. My mother will not like this.

A dab of spit takes care of the smudge. I find my comb and do the best I can to look like I have a hairdo. How did she know I was here? Maternal instinct? That makes me laugh. Who cares how she knew? She's here.

*I don't understand why I'm so happy.*

*I should be pissed off.*

*She came to find me.*

*Maybe something bad happened.*

*Then she wouldn't be smiling.*

*She's looking around for me.*

*Why does this feel so good?*

She stops at the fence that separates the basketball court from the playground. She glances to the side, not toward me but at the metal picnic tables. A small girl squeals and runs past her, another right behind, playing tag. She follows their path, then goes back to her search.

*Just a sec, Mom,* I want to yell.

I dig in my backpack for a clean T-shirt and slip it on, stuffing my dirty one down into the front pouch.

My heart's going to pound right out of my chest. I do a final check and stand up. I nod, like someone's spoken to me, blink against the sun, and emerge from my nook. Should I bring my backpack? If I'm going home, will I need it? I opt for bring. I leave my blanket, figuring

I'll toss it through the fence later, or just leave it for the next kid who needs a corner in the park to sleep. But how will I let Coco know that I've gone?

I wonder how she got here. Did she drive? Is Marianne with her, waiting in the car? Or maybe my dad? I suddenly feel like crying, which would be dumb since I'm totally happy. My mother finally understands. In the back of my mind, I always knew she would. You don't just stop loving your son, no matter what. She's probably been looking for me since before I left the city.

It just took all this time —

She turns toward me, takes a step, and lifts her hand to wave. I lift mine to wave back. She drops the other hand from her forehead, and two little boys scamper out from the park building. She crouches down and opens her arms. They run in for a hug, laughing and talking, then speed off for the jungle gym. A man follows the boys and she stands to hug him.

"Look at me, Mommy, look at me!" the big boy yells, hanging upside down from the bar.

I keep waving.

I pretend there's a friend calling me.

I shake my head back and forth, like my friend has asked a question and I have to say no. I keep the smile because, what else is there to do? My insides are crumbling, and my face twitches, weirdly, like I've been shocked by electrical wires. I think of the ants and how they kept moving. I call up my mother's real face, the one she showed me the last time we were together — mean and old and ugly.

I take a breath. Turn, walk the few steps back. My body seems wrapped in cloth, even my face now, like a shroud. I'm aware of every inch of skin. I roll up my blanket and shove it through the metal gate, under the ivy. I munch on the muffin Coco gave me last night, slightly worse for the squishing it got inside my backpack. I change back to the dirty shirt; I'll dress up later when I go to work. I decide I'll get food first, and find Coco; we can go play somewhere or maybe just sit and hug and talk. Until right this second, I didn't realize how hungry I am. A strawberry shake sounds pretty damn good. I sling the backpack over my shoulder and strut out across the playground.

On the tip-top of the structure, the little boys pretend to be flying a plane.

"Pilot to co-pilot," the bigger one says to the smaller. The woman laughs with them. The man sees me and moves to stand between his kids and where I'll pass.

I want to scream at him — *Don't worry! I'm fourteen, I can't hurt you, what's your problem* — instead I keep my eyes level and on the street ahead. When the woman follows her husband's gaze, I can't help myself. For a quick second, I look directly at her. Her smile changes to a scowl. Her eyes get wary, scared, like a dog who's going to be struck. I was wrong. She doesn't even *resemble* my mother, except of course for the black hair and that expression, the one that accuses me of being something horrible.

I flip her off and laugh as her face turns red.

The sun makes me blink. I shade my eyes. My stomach growls. Maybe I'll get a Big Mac with that shake.

You know who your friends are by who sticks around when the going gets tough. It's a jungle now, no two ways about that. L.A.'s no place for the weak-minded and being Punk carries a significant responsibility. It doesn't fucking matter how much we fight each other — whether we come from the Inland Empire or fucking Orange County. What matters is that we stick up for ourselves.

Always.

Regardless.

The outside world pokes a nose in, that nose is gonna get broke.

I feel the vibe before I get out of the house that afternoon. Something's up, out there in the world, coming at me, fast. I just don't know what. I keep an eye on my dad when he drives up from work. Not because he scares me anymore, just this other sense of things. On my way down to meet Jack, I keep looking over my shoulder. What the fuck, huh? Too much coke last night? Who knows. But I'm not ignoring it. Gotta keep on your toes. You never know when something's gonna bite.

Around four, I head up to the gas station on Santa Monica and Highland and lounge along the wall to wait for some paying customer to get the key to the bathroom. They've recently put in locks and you have to get the key from the skinny Arab at the cash register. Who takes great pleasure in never giving it to one of us.

It doesn't take long.

A dad brings his little boy in; I get the look, I shrug it off. Who cares? What do they know about anything anyway? When they come out, I slip in, lock the door, strip down and give myself a good wash. The water's freezing but it feels like heaven to have my hair clean. I still don't wear underwear; I doubt if I'd like it now. I roll up my jeans and T-shirt and pack them away.

I blot myself dry with paper towels, style my hair with soap gel and the hand dryer, take a piss, and slip into my evening attire. My pants are tight. My butt looks good. With my boots, I stand long and lean, like a pencil. I figure I must be almost five-five now. And last, but not least, I unbutton my shirt a bit. I think how Coco likes to put his cheek on my chest.

It's hard to see myself clearly. The mirror isn't glass, it's metal and pretty scratched up. Still and all — not too bad. Not too bad at all. I smile, drop my head down in that flirty way I do, practice peering up from underneath my eyelashes. Good butt, great lashes, long and thick, and of course — my beautiful eyes. People still tell me I've got beautiful eyes.

At least my mother gave me something.

Jack feels it too, I can tell. He's edgy. Not that he's ever *calm*, but now he can't stay still. Keeps flipping through tapes, can't settle in to one. We stop at Rosie's. Her eyes are smudged when she gets in the car.

"What happened?" I ask.

"Nothing. It's okay." She pushes my hand away when I try to turn her toward me. "Let's just go."

Jack starts to pull off, but I stop him. "Your mom home?"

Rosie shakes her head no.

"I'm fine, let's go, let's just go."

Maybe this is it, what I've been feeling. Frank chooses just that second to peek out through the curtains. I don't say another word. I get out and go to the door. I hear him put the chain lock on, but this is a cheap apartment. One big kick and whole thing busts open.

"I told you, didn't I?"

"Doug, look —"

"You think I'm stupid?"

He doesn't get another word out. I pop him, just once, right in the center of his nose — HARD. I hear the sucker break. I shake my hand out. Rosie's smiling when I get back in the car.

I feel my old self returning. That woman was an omen, and a reminder — a good one. Things are going to change for the better. One last check in the bathroom mirror. Yep. I look good tonight. Really good. It's Thursday, and Thursdays are never slow, so I won't get bored.

Tonight could be the night.

It's already starting to feel different.

Tonight could be when I finally meet that someone who's going to make a difference. Slender, not too tall, not too old, and good-looking. Definitely good-looking, in a rugged kind of way. He'll have dark hair and beautiful eyes, like mine, except maybe brown or blue. He'll like Coco too. He'll be the one to see who I really am.

Wasted Youth, Black Flag, the Stains, and MAD Society, with eight-year-old singer "Stevie," are at the Polish Hall. We're rocking the place when the cops show up and warn us they might have to shut it down. Greg Ginn takes the mic.

"All right, people, let's be *reasonable* and show L.A.'s *FINEST* we're just here to play. We're here to *play*. Always just *here-to-play*. You with me?" Any more sarcasm and even the walls would get it.

A roar goes up. The crowd approves. The cops stay cool. We stay cool. They don't move too fast, we don't go overboard on anybody. It's a sweet kind of tension, like right before you come.

Then a little Punk girl gets pushed into a cop, who looks like a kid himself. A scared kid. He shoves her off of him. Hard. Says: *get your funky ass off me, bitch*. She pops him, square in the nose. It starts to bleed. Rosie and I hoot. His partner whirls and smacks the girl with his nightstick. Her boyfriend punches him.

That's it. We're off. All of us.

Bottles, rocks, anything we can find goes flying through the air. Everybody cuts loose. We hit cops, we hit each other, some guy jumps on the stage and flings himself on top of the crowd. He falls through to the ground and a cop gets him good with his stick. All hell's breaking out and I'm right in the thick of it. Taking hits from all sides and giving back even more.

Heaven.

Then the cops chuck tear gas inside and all bets are off. I get it directly in one eye. I can't see, my nose runs, my lungs are on fire. All around, people drop to the floor—throwing up, coughing, screaming about their eyes. No choice but *get out*. We elbow through the doorway and into a corridor of cops, a fucking wall of blue uniforms and night sticks. Cattle herded down a chute. A Punk who's fallen reaches up to grab me. I keep hold of Rosie with one hand and punch him with the other, to make him let go.

Now Rosie's leading me, I can't keep my eyes open. We make it to Jack's car and tumble into the backseat.

"You okay, Dougie?" Rosie asks, trying to peer into my eye. I nod. Shit, yeah, I'm okay. I got this bitter taste going down my throat from the gas, or maybe from the Black Beauties we snorted earlier, but I'm amped and racing. Wanting more. Every nerve's on edge.

We hit Sunset. Some bitch in the front seat lights one of those stupid clove cigarettes. Now I really want to hit somebody. I hate that smell. Another girl, Chloe, wears that cinnamony patchouli hippie crap. I hate that too. I roll down the window, take a huge swallow from the bottle of peppermint schnapps I found tucked under the seat. Rosie leans on my arm. I start to be able to open my eyes.

It's a Thursday; the street's packed with tourists and locals, Punks, jocks, stoners, hippies, lots of hookers. Girl hookers. They strut back and

forth with their little tight skirts and big asses hanging out. They make
faces at us. Especially the black ones. One girl flips her skirt up at us.

"S my D, bitch, S my D!" Jack yells.

Chloe's saved three big bags of french fries with ketchup and relish
on them. She leans across me and Rosie to throw it at the hooker on
the corner when we stop at the light. She misses. I grab one and hit the
bitch dead on. Everybody laughs and the hooker cops an attitude.
Takes a step, like she's so black and tough, she can actually do something. Jack hits the brakes.

Rosie's all over it. "Got something to say, bitch?"

She flips us off and me and Rosie start toward her, fast. She turns on
her stupid high heels and runs toward the hookers across the street. I
chuck the last bag of fries—bull's-eye! Two cars behind us, some Punks
from the concert honk their horns and yell. Me and Rosie climb back in
the car, share the schnapps, settle back in the seat. I still want more.

So Wonder-Guy Sugar Daddy doesn't show up that night, but it's okay,
because I don't get arrested either. In fact, I make a few bucks and
nothing bad happens and I actually have a real cutie tell me he wants to
see me again. I meet up with Timmy at Astro Burger around two.

"Let's go across the street," he says. "I'm craving Oki Dogs." Jesse
and Coco catch up with us as we're crossing. I smile to myself. You
have to keep perspective, that's all it takes. Coco drops his arm around
me, gives me a kiss on the cheek.

"My treat," he whispers.

"You want some shit?" the counter guy says. He always says that.
"I make you some good shit!"

I order one, Coco gets two, and we settle into the little room to eat.

The first time I saw an Oki Dog, I thought it was gross. I mean, two hot dogs slopped with chili and pastrami, wrapped together in a tortilla? Ew. Now I love them. I take my first bite and realize I haven't eaten since the afternoon. I polish it off, lean back, hands behind my head, legs stretched and crossed in front of me.

"Who's got quarters?" Jesse asks, hanging on to Timmy. Coco hands over a couple and the two of them go to play Pac-Man. We settle on the bench in the little arcade area.

"What are you smiling about?" Coco asks.

"I'm happy." This is my family now. What more could I want?

Jack pulls into the parking lot across from Oki Dogs. A beat-up green Volkswagen bumps us from behind, people pile out, some guy catapults himself on top of our car and slides to the ground. Another guy comes over and kicks him. They get into it. I light a cigarette.

"Well, shit," Jack mutters. "Look at that." He points across the street to Oki Dogs. "Look where all the faggots are."

The tussling stops and people stand up to check it out. Nobody in Astro Burger tonight. That would be okay; we don't bother the whores there. But Oki Dogs belongs to us. Our tribe. Our streets. Our way.

A black Corvair swerves in, more Punks pile out. My tribe gathers.

"Faggot whores," Jack whispers.

I feel myself swelling.

"Let's get 'em." Voices in the crowd. "Let's kill the faggots." "Tonight the faggots die."

"Kill the faggots!" I say. It goes to a chant. The light's red, we cross anyway. Our boots rock the street.

*Kill the faggots.*

My heart skips a beat; I open my eyes.

"So this guy," Coco's saying, his mouth full, "looks so much like my Uncle Jeffie I think my mom's got to be in the backseat and —"

*"Kill the faggots!"*

We all freeze. Pac-Man beeps on his own. I drop my legs and stand to see Mohawks and leather jackets crossing the street, marching toward us. An army in silhouette, at least a hundred of them. My legs tremble. Laser beams shoot from their eyes, slice through night.

They scatter like cockroaches, scrambling in all directions. We spread out. I angle along the parking lot side. Jack goes around. The counter guy stares. I flip him off and yell, "YOU WANT SOME GOOD SHIT, ASSHOLE?" He drops his head, gets real busy.

I know I'm running but it's taking forever. I can't seem to reach the alley and when I do — the skinheads appear, their laser eyes trapping me. Everything blurs. I should have thought, I should have known, I should have been careful. *God, are you there?*

Kill the faggots!

We split up and close in, like a military tactic, shutting off all sides. Two faggots bolt; people chase them. The other two are trapped. One's on the ground. I almost step on him. Another tries for the alley.

A hand whirls me around. Boots thud on flesh; I hear grunts in reply. Is that me? Coco yells, "Nazi assholes!" I try to yell too, but I get punched in my stomach and all my air disappears. I double over, can't speak, can't run. Is Jesus watching?

The first one fights like crazy. He calls us names, throws punches, lands a direct kick on Jack's knee so hard it makes him stumble back. In that one second—the faggot's up and running. Gone. I've never seen anything run that fast.

No faces. Only hands, pulling and shoving me; only feet, kicking so hard I drop to my knees, cradle my head in my arms. Is this it? Voices yelling "FAGGOT! FAGGOT!" Thuds, grunts, chains jangling as boots connect to my thigh, to my back, shoulder, legs, head, arms. "FAG-GOT!!" A siren somewhere far. Coco, getting away. *"FAGGOT!!!"*

That chemical crap still floats in the back of my throat. My lips are dry, my head pounds from the fucking tear gas. I'm amped, like speeding on the freeway, zooming through those tunnels on the 110 where you curve around way too fast and the wall's way too close and you don't slow down.

These must be demons my mother's sent to punish me. I taste blood inside my mouth, around my teeth. I pull my knees to my chest. I pee my pants. Why don't the boots hurt? Am I dead?

Sirens closing in. This is taking too long. These Punks are too slow. I get into the circle to see the kid. The faggot. He's curled up on his side, crying. *"He's not out yet?! SHIT. Can't you fuckers handle this?"*

I hear one voice above the others and something makes me raise my head. The biggest demon of all stands with his face in half shadow, laser eyes boring down. I can't look away.

Fucking faggot looks dead at me. Reflex, habit—I don't think, I just kick him, once, hard—right in the face. Be done with it. His head snaps back and forth, drops, lays against the street. Blood leaks and pools on the concrete. I remember the razor blade tucked into the toe of my boot.

Time stops, like it did in the hall inside the dance school, like it did in the moment of my mother's face.

We stand at the edge of the light under that street lamp in the alley, and for a moment, nobody moves. I don't even breathe. I hear my heart. Stupid little shit.

*See how you like living with perverts.*

You got to stand up for yourself.

*You're not my brother anymore.*

You can't let the faggot whores take over.

*No child of mine is a faggot.*

You have to fight for what you believe.

God, his eyes are blue.

# AFTER

The kid's not moving.

Jack grabs my arm, pulls me away.

We run. Back across the street, jump in the cars.

People whoop and cheer.

Some girl keeps saying "Oh my god you guys are fucked — that's so fucked, you guys, oh my god, oh my god —" on and on and ON until she's making me sick and finally, somebody tells her to shut up and she shuts up. I don't know how I get in the car, but I'm here, in the backseat, Rosie holding onto my arm. We race down Hollywood Boulevard and past the graveyard, the car bouncing hard. We take the on-ramp too fast and everybody slides into me. I don't even care.

"You think he's okay?" Rosie whispers. "That kid?"

"How the fuck should I know?"

"You sure drop-kicked that faggot, Doug!" Jack says. He pounds on the steering wheel. "Whomp! Down! End of story! That faggot's history. Out of here. Gone."

Then it's quiet. Not usual. We should be bragging, all of us. But no-body has anything to say. Tonight was different. Tonight we . . .

I take out my flask. It's empty.

"Dougie, you think he's dead?" Rosie whispers.

"Stop asking me stupid questions!" I hiss at her, then tap Jack's shoulder. "Turn up the fucking music, would you?" He does, without protest, which is weird. What's weirder is Rosie stops yapping. She slumps down in the seat and stares out the window.

My mom pops her face out of her room as I come in, then pulls back, like a turtle into its shell. The jet plane in my head pushes on my skull. I grab the Jack Daniels from the liquor cabinet and drink from the bottle, right there in the living room. Let her peek her head out now. The burn feels good; I drink again. I carry it up to my room. I strip off my shirt and sit on the bed to unlace my boots. Bending forward makes me dizzy and suddenly nauseous. I'll undress in the morning. I drink more and then lay back.

*Is he dead?*

*So what if he is. What am I supposed I do about it?*

*Nothing.*

There's nothing *to* do. I don't know for sure. He could be fine. He could be getting his buddies together, coming after me. I can't go back and look. Whatever happened, happened. It's over. Done.

I throw up. It doesn't help. I can't stop seeing his stupid eyes.

*Why did he have to look up at me?*

*Why did I kick him so hard?*

*What does it fucking matter anyway?*

*He shouldn't have been there in the first place.*

Light glows through haze.

I can't feel my body or tell if my eyes are open.

*Is it God? Am I dead?*

Then I breathe and pain slices through my side like razors slashing, glass piercing, so huge I can only pant, try to suck in tiny bits of air through my nose. *Am I stabbed?* I lift my head to see but I can only open one eye; the world tilts and whirls and then —

Sun. My head throbbing. Pain with each breath. Still only one eye will open. I creep my arm up to touch my side — more pain, a ripple of nausea. My ribs must be broken. I try to lay still, but somehow do a check. I wiggle my toes, flex my feet, slowly draw up my right knee. I seem able to move my arm, but my leg feels like it might be broken too. Lumps are already rising.

A single crow caws from the power line overhead. A garbage can in the parking lot clangs shut. A guy whistles. Someone from Oki Dogs? I taste blood in my mouth, move my tongue over my teeth. None gone, but a tooth has punctured the inside of my lip. I hear people walk past me on the sidewalk. I can't draw the breath to call out.

I remember boots and shouts.

Coco, running.

The skinheads. *What if they come back?*

I need to get up, I need to go. I count ONE, TWO, and on THREE, heave myself to sit. The crow cries out. No, it's not the bird, it's me. The top of a cop car cruises by. Doesn't slow. It's my left eye that won't open. Tiny pebbles stick to the side of my face. I brush off the stones and bleed again.

*He's not out yet?*

I hear that voice, see those blue eyes. He wanted me to be dead. They all did.

A chill goes up my spine.

I stand, slowly, using the concrete barrier to balance. I throw up, there's blood mixed in. I'm dizzy, feel like I'm going faint, except I can't.

So I don't.

My right leg almost collapses when I step on it. I hop on the other leg and make it across to the wall, then have to wait. The edges of my vision close down, like a telescope. I limp over to Santa Monica Boulevard. I put my head down, wrap my arms around my sides, concentrate on putting one foot in front of the other. I have several blocks to go and each step makes me want to weep. People pass me. Their faces go blank, like I'm not here.

Maybe I'm not. Maybe it's all a bad dream.

I see myself in a store window. Stop for a second to make sure that yes, I exist. I keep moving.

The attendant at the gas station glares as I pass his window. He comes out a few minutes later to check if I've gone; I hide behind a parked car. When someone who's allowed to have the bathroom key comes out, I catch the door, go in, and lock it.

My forehead is split to the bone; dried blood glues my eye shut. I'm dizzy again. I put my hands on the sink, wait. It passes. I need stitches and antiseptic; I should go to the clinic or maybe the hospital. Who cares if they call the police? Nothing would be worse than this.

Except —

A memory surfaces, fully formed, in grand detail.

A memory I'd stopped, the very night it happened: my mother and me, in that room, the cop and therapist next door.

First I hear her words: "No child of mine is a faggot."

But it's not those words I forgot, or the slap that knocked me down. It was the second just before — the moment she *disconnected*. When the light changed in her eyes and she stopped being . . . what? My mom? When she became —

Just like the skinheads.

I feel a pain greater than my broken ribs and I know, if I die, it will be this that kills me. My heart is breaking. I know something I desperately need to forget. Whatever it costs, I can't see those eyes again; I will not survive.

No clinic.

I can take care of myself. I wash the wound with the soap from the dispenser. At 7-Eleven, I get gauze, tape, and Neosporin. I pull the edges of skin together, make a bandage and tape it shut. I keep my head up as I limp back to the park. I challenge people's eyes in that instant before they look away. If I see it coming, I can take care of myself. I notice signs for the first time: DON'T WALK. NO STOPPING. NO LOITERING. NO STANDING. FOR CUSTOMERS ONLY. *NO BEAT-UP BOYS ALLOWED*.

In my nook, I tear my bloody shirt into strips and wrap those around my rib cage, like I saw my dad do once when he took a header off his bike. It hurts too much not to cry. A woman walking a dog stops to stare. I wait. Will she help? Speak? Say, "Honey, are you okay?" No, she moves on. It doesn't matter. I'll be all right.

But, I will never, ever, see my mother again. I know this.

I know something else too — I'm here for a reason.

I must be, or I'd be dead.

The next day's easier. My head pounds but I know the remedy for that. Both my parents are gone already, so the liquor's all mine. I change my clothes, shower, eat a piece of toast, get a nice buzz going. I won't go to school, just mellow out. Maybe later I'll go check out Stacie. I heard Carlos left. I'm sure as hell done with Barbies.

I settle down on my parents' bed and flip on the TV. Only once do I think of last night, and immediately see that faggot's green eyes. He asked for it, sure as shit. My head starts to roar. I go get another drink, almost straight bourbon with a little splash of Coke. I guess I fall asleep because the next thing I know, my father's there, poking at me.

"Get the hell off my bed," he says.

"Fuck you," I say, before I really even come to. I don't mean to say it, but I'm not sorry; he woke me up. What does he expect?

"What did you say, you stupid shit?" comes out at the same time he grabs me and slings me off the bed. But I'm not my brother, and I'm sure as hell not small, and even though he manages to get me on the floor, it's not but two seconds before I'm back up and in his face. I don't care how bad my hip hurts, it's nothing compared to what I look for and take, every single day. I don't bother cussing him, I get down to business. I haul off and punch my father in the face. He slams up against the wall. I punch him again and hear something crack. Then Mom's yelling, "Stop it, stop it, you'll hurt him!" But this time she's yelling at me, not at him. This time, it's my boot in his ass instead of the other way around.

Coco comes to find me.

"Oh, honey," he says, waking me, gently touching my face. "Oh, babe, I'm so sorry." He's crying. Timmy's with him and a man I don't know. They take me out of Plummer Park, over to a room where the man says we can stay, at least for a while.

I lay in the bed for three days. Coco brings me food. He rubs my feet. He gives me a sponge bath, at least as much as I can take. He doesn't try to make me go to the hospital. He helps me change my bandage and clean out the wound. It doesn't get infected. We watch the bruises turn black and green all down one side of my leg and body. Coco makes jokes about me turning Martian. He gets painkillers and Valium from one of his tricks.

I heal.

We move from the room and find a new place to stay, in a different park, someplace where we can meet up with each other every night. I love this boy. He's my angel.

I wait as long as we can manage, then take my working clothes and hike down to a new gas station to clean up. Coco doesn't try to talk me out of it. I change. I gel my hair, combing it over in a curl to one side to cover the Band-Aid. Tricks don't like to know you can get hurt.

I get ready and check myself out. This bathroom has a real mirror. I look okay, except something's different. I can't put my finger on what it is. I check myself out on all sides, still can't see it. But something's changed.

"You look fine to me," Coco says, giving me a kiss.

I don't do so good at first. I'm too scared. I wave tricks off. I always need to make sure someone knows where I am. I hold on to the door handle the whole time.

"It's okay, babe," Coco says. "You don't need to. We're fine. Don't worry."

But we're not, so little by little, I make myself work again. New areas. I won't go near Oki Dogs. Seeing a Punk or a skinhead makes my whole body shake. My bruises fade and disappear. The scar on my head does not. I keep combing my hair in a little curl over the top of it.

The street's changing. There's a gay disease nobody can explain and lots of cocaine. People are meaner, paranoid about everything. I won't ever do drugs when I'm working. I'm very careful. Even so, I get arrested a couple of times. I tell them I'm Paul, so I do a few days and don't have to go to Juvie. Tricks never get busted, just the kids.

Coco finds a sugar daddy and moves to Long Beach. He invites me to come along, but it wouldn't work. I start hanging out at clubs when I can; I look older now and it's not hard to get in. I don't tell anyone what I do. I flirt and glance up at guys from under my lashes.

Me and a bunch of working boys get an apartment east of Vine a few blocks off Hollywood Boulevard. I start meeting people in the clubs. I drink there, probably too much, but it's fun. I get to make up stories and be whoever I feel like being. Sometimes I'm JJ, starving actor.

"Great bone structure," says a handsome young guy at Akiko's Lounge. "You could model, easy. If the acting thing doesn't work out, you know?"

This makes me happy. At home, I stand looking at myself in the bathroom mirror, fixing my hair over my scar, checking out my bone structure. It is pretty good. I lower my head and peer up through my lashes, then freeze.

I see it, that change I noticed before. It's my eyes. They're as green as ever, but something's gone. I turn one way, then the other, but I can't make them beautiful. Not anymore.

*        *        *

Angels come in all forms, and this one is dark-haired with light hazel eyes. I meet him at Akiko's and something clicks. Within the week, I move into his apartment. I'm seventeen. He's twenty-six. I'm off the streets, the first time in four years. I keep expecting to wake up and have him put me out, but he doesn't. Finally, I tell him the truth about myself. He says he already knows. He doesn't care. He loves me. He makes me enroll in beauty school. I learn to color hair. I'm good at it.

His name is Curtis.

Curtis.

I like how it rolls off my tongue. I like him. A lot. Pretty soon, I think I love him. I get a job as a colorist — my first ever "real" job.

My first ever real family.

Life is good.

# 1989

## NINE YEARS AFTER

"You see what I'm saying?"

The kid nods. He's a scrawny boy, with eyes that dart about constantly, like he's keeping a lookout for whatever might be coming to get him. Tattoos everywhere; the one that says MOM with the image of a gun worked in catches my eye. He's always by himself. Nineteen, maybe twenty. Needy. Scared.

I've had my eye on him for a while. It's time to see if he's open to the doctrine. I never push anyone. I'm ready to back right off if he's the least bit afraid of it. You got to be open to hearing the truth, or it's a waste of time. I wasn't pushed, I didn't have to be. By the time I started listening to the skinheads, *really listening*—the message came through loud and clear. I got set straight, put on the path. White people have got to take care of themselves. We don't need to hurt anybody, unless they step over bounds, but we have got to keep our guard up.

"You're not alone in this," I say, kinda low, so the "people" standing nearby aren't going to hear us. There's lots of "people" around in

Hollywood nowadays, and they take every chance they find to mess with kids like this boy I'm talking to right now.

Cassie comes up then, smiling, as beautiful as ever, with her buzz cut and deep dark eyes. Sexy girl—and all mine. One hundred percent White Racialist, we met at a rally out in El Monte. I still can't believe she fell for me.

"Hey," she says to the kid. "Hungry?"

"Kinda," he answers, and I can see him trying not to be too obvious in checking her out.

"Come on, then, let's get you something to eat."

We go to the new Oki Dogs, the one down on Fairfax. Cassie orders. I fill him in on how it used to be for Punks in Hollywood, and all the shit we used to do at the other Oki Dogs.

"That's before the fag whores took over," I explain.

I find out his story—single mom, abusive stepdad, never fit in, got beat up by cholos at his high school, hardcore drugs. His life sucks and people have told him it's all his fault. He's ready. We talk. Cassie and me set him up to meet some people and then we are done. We send him off smiling, knowing he's not alone. We feel good.

It's getting dark when we get back to Pomona.

"Let's get some beers, huh?" I say, turning into the little market near our house. Cassie hops out and sprints across to the door. The girl's closed it, is just finished turning the key, when Cassie gets there.

"Come on—just one thing, huh?" she asks.

"No, no, *señorita*, we closed now."

"Please?" Cassie smiles and tilts her head to the side, makes her eyes big. Drives me crazy when she does that.

"*Lo siento mucho.* We closed."

"Pretty pretty please? We just want a six-pack. We had a really hard day at work."

I see the girl waver, smile, and then click back the key. The second she opens the door, Cassie snatches the front of her shirt and pulls her outside. The girl screams and Cassie slaps her, sends her sprawling to her knees on the ground. "You be still, you hear, SEEN YOUR RITA?" She marches in and grabs the Coors. Doesn't pay. I laugh all the way home.

# 1989

## NINE YEARS AFTER

"Look at those poor little boys."

I do, peering out of the back of the limo. I'm with Jay, my assistant. We're driving down Santa Monica Boulevard, actually going by the old Oki Dogs. A boy is perched on the very same bench where I used to — I stop myself.

That's the old life.

Gone.

Over.

Forgotten.

Nobody in my world now knows a thing about it. I'm a colorist. I do stars. I fly all over the country, go on location. I'm on my way to FOX Studios tonight, command performance, so to speak. There's a night shoot; my star needs her hair touched up.

"I think I'd rather die than do that," Jay says.

"No kidding," I say.

# 1998

EIGHTEEN YEARS AFTER
SEVEN YEARS BEFORE

"Look, Daddy! There's one!"

My daughter's shrill six-year-old voice cuts right through the noise in the supermarket. People stop, look over at us. We're in the checkout line: the basket's full. The twins are standing up, one on each side, holding onto the shopping cart, proud that they don't have to sit inside or in the baby seat. The store's crowded—it's close to Thanksgiving. Turkey decorations are everywhere. Everybody around turns toward us, smiling, wondering what these cute little blond kids have seen.

"Where? Where? Where?" Nicolas pipes in.

"There!" Andy reaches over and pats Nick. "See? Right there!" She tugs at my arm and points to a big woman in the front of the line. "That's sure a black nigger, huh, Daddy?"

"That's a *black* nigger all right," Nick agrees.

The woman she's talking about looks straight at me. Her smile fades. Her eyes flash dark and angry. She shakes her head. The air in the store sizzles. No one speaks. A black man who already checked out turns around, edges past the woman and starts walking toward us. I don't say a word. I pick my kids up off of the cart and sling each one under an arm. We march toward the entrance doors. I don't look anywhere but forward. I'm six-four, wearing a wifebeater, with a shaved head and arms full of Neo-Nazi and White Power tattoos. I'm no skinny kid now; I work out and it shows. I know how to walk tough. I put my mean face on. I'm not bullshitting. People move out of my way.

Except the black guy. He follows.

"Hey! Racist Asshole!" he yells and I turn my head to see how close he is, if I should run. I never would, on my own, but I got my kids now; their welfare comes first.

He's a lucky man. If they weren't here —

For a second, our eyes lock. A firestorm of pure anger connects us. For a second, the rest of the world goes away. We recognize each other, draw the line, throw down the gauntlet. It could go either way. He hates me every bit as much as I hate him.

"Don't bother," the woman says, coming up beside him, placing a hand on his arm. "Just feel sorry for those kids. They ain't got a chance in hell."

"You got that right," he answers. He looks like he wants to do us some serious damage.

"The sins of the fathers," the woman adds. "God help those poor babies."

I get to the truck and swing the twins inside the cab.

"I wanna ride in the back!" Nicolas says. "You said we could!" Andrea joins in, "Pleasepleaseplease!!!"

"Both of you shut up and get in there!"

I don't mean to sound as harsh as I do. But they don't know what almost happened, what still might. They don't understand how very bad this whole thing could turn out. Andrea starts to whimper.

"What's wrong, Daddy?" she asks. "Why did we leave all our stuff?"

"Don't worry about it," I snap, and her face crumples.

"Are we still having Thanksgiving?" she moans.

"Yes. Now be still." That old jet plane starts to rev. Makes it hard to concentrate on them and this situation at the same time.

She starts to whimper; Nick's not far behind. I can't care right now. I need to get them out of here. I saw that man's eyes. I know what he's capable of doing.

The woman's words come up: "The sins of the father"? What the hell is that supposed to mean?

"I want my ice cream," Nick whines. "Can I have my ice cream?"

"That was *my* ice cream!" Andrea says.

"Was not."

"Was so!"

They argue as I buckle them in and back the truck out of the parking space, keeping an eye on the crowd that's gathering. Not good. Not good at all. This shit could explode any second. My kids are in danger—these two tiny beings I love like I never have loved anything in my entire life. I have put them at risk. Fear as big as the whole fucking universe surrounds me. I've never felt this, ever—not in the worst time, not even with my dad.

I have never been this scared.

I have never had so much at stake.

These are my babies. My world.

The black guy stands in front of the store, glaring at us. Does he have a gun? A bunch of other black guys have joined him. White guys too. Probably Jews. The woman's gone. What if they decide to attack? My head roars with possibilities. They got cars, they could chase us, catch us, even now. Riots have started with less provocation.

It's taking forever to get through the parking lot. What if they rush me, pull me out of the cab? I'll fight like hell for my kids, but there's more of them than there are of me and I'm not packing. I never do when I have the twins. What if those assholes shoot me? If my kids see me die? What if they shoot my kids?

I flash on Cassie, years ago, when they first were born. She'd seen a picture of my great-uncle, from France, with his dark French skin.

"You better know this now," she'd threatened. "If there's once ounce of dark blood in those babies, I'll bash both their heads against the wall. I will. I swear it."

I tried to laugh it off, because I knew she couldn't be serious. Doctrine's one thing, blood's another. She carried them inside her, went through fifteen hours of labor to give them birth. But that night, I watched her face as she got Nick and Andy ready for bed. She picked them up like she was picking up dogshit. When Andy squirmed in reaction, Cassie shook her, hard. Andy started to cry, which got Nick going too. I took them both outside for a walk.

Hate is possible in anyone.

Hate is full of power.

Hate makes you feel invincible, strong, capable of fighting all your enemies. It wraps itself around your biggest fears and makes those fears go away.

Suddenly the faces of the Iranian couple from years ago flash in my head, how they looked before we beat them up. I get a rush of the absolute power I felt at seeing that. At knowing their fear of me was so huge, I did not need to feel afraid of them.

I was in charge, I had the power.

They would do anything to escape.

Just like I would, right now.

If it were just me, and that man attacked, or even the whole crowd of them did—I wouldn't care. I'm still not afraid of pain. Or dying. I don't give a fuck who beats my head in, as long as I get my chance to beat them back.

But how could my children survive this world without me? What if they'd been alone? Maybe a little older? What if they'd said that word, just like they'd been taught, like they'd always heard at home, from us, from our friends, in our meetings? What would have happened to them then?

*"The sins of the father . . ."*

I have put my children in danger.

*"God help those babies."*

I take the turn by the little market and remember the girl who opened the door for Cassie. Whose fault was that? Hers for trusting? Or Cassie's? The rest of the drive home, I count the faces of people who are not white. Tons. Then I think of all the white people who are different than us. The gays. The Catholics. There are so many people my kids have learned to hate. So many people that will now hate them back.

I thought I was protecting them.

"Daddy!" Nicolas yells, "Andy pinched me!"

I glance over and instead of my own sweet-faced son, I see another boy. A boy with green eyes, instead of Nicky's sparkling blue. He was years older than my children, but still—a *boy*. He looked directly at me—terrified, and for an instant, impossibly bold. He knew something and it pissed me off. He understood what I am just now, this very minute, finding out.

It has to do with fear and hate.

And children.

And hope.

It changes everything. It changes me.

The cab's downstairs, the cabbie's honked twice. My plane leaves in an hour. Meanwhile, the television blares from the living room. If I'd turned it off an hour ago — oh well. I shove the suitcase off the bed and sit on top to close it. Curtis could have done this, easy, but he had to leave before I'd finished packing.

"It's only three days, babe," he teased, watching me drag things out of the closet, "not three months."

"Yes, but you never know what my little star might decide she needs to do." I looked up at him from under my lashes, and his eyes crinkled as he smiled. I stood on tiptoes to give him a kiss.

"Good luck, sweetie," he said. "I love you."

"I love you too."

I bounce on the suitcase, and click, it's latched. The cabbie honks again and I sigh; press junkets used to be exciting. Now I can't wait to come home. I lug the case down the hall, past our recently remodeled bathroom, my birthday present from Curtis, which makes me smile. In the living room, I call out the window to the cabbie, signal two minutes and snatch the TV remote. I point it just as the screen gives way to "Breaking News."

A young man's photo appears. Nineteen, maybe twenty, I can't tell. Sweet-faced and sad-eyed, slight, he reminds me of my older brother, Paul. Strange, I haven't thought of my family for years.

The boy was discovered tied to a fence, unconscious.

"I thought it was a scarecrow," says the guy who found him. "Until I got close and saw the blood."

I don't know this boy, yet my hand, still aiming the remote, begins to shake uncontrollably. I have to think to lower it. My legs tremble. My heart pounds so violently it seems to be rattling my chest. The cabbie leans on the horn, I jerk my head toward the window but my eyes won't leave the screen. I step back, stumble over the suitcase, manage to catch myself and sit on the edge of the couch. I hear the cab screech away and don't care. So I miss my flight. So I get fired.

The boy's a college student. He'd been at a bar. The bartender talked with him awhile, then saw him leave with two men he didn't seem to know.

They think these two men beat him up, drove him out to the countryside, and left him on the fence to die.

Tied there, like an animal.

They think it was done because the boy is gay.

I make it to my new bathroom just in time. I throw up my breakfast, rinse out my mouth, go back to the TV. I can't turn it off. A key sounds in the door; Curtis rushes in. He sits down beside me.

"It's too awful, isn't it?" he says. "Are you okay?"

I shake my head no and he wraps me inside his arms. We huddle close, glued to the screen. We hear the story again and again: Matthew Shepard was beaten with a pistol. He was tied to a fence in the middle of the night, bleeding, in freezing weather. He was left there to die.

By people he did not even know.

Because he is gay.

Curtis is saying something — I see his lips move, but don't hear the words. I see the TV screen flash on the hospital where Matthew Shepard is now in intensive care, but my mind has gone to another boy, lying on the ground in a spot I recognize immediately but haven't remembered until now.

He too was beaten and left.

I hear him cry out as he lifts himself up. I walk with him as he stumbles down the alley, supporting himself on fences and cars and

the backs of the buildings. I watch him turn onto the street, I see people pass him, watch as their eyes glaze over, turn away, render him
invisible.

He leans in toward a store window and stares at his own reflection.
What does he see?

I remember clearly.

I saw a person who could survive anything, a person strong enough
to take care of himself.

Now, I see a little boy. Fourteen. A child.

As the newscast continues, I play through that night, recalling what I
felt, what I thought, how everything that happened went so quickly out
of control.

*"Kill the faggots!"*

I remember the skinheads, the sounds of their boots. Them, chant-
ing. Me, running. Coco's screams. How none of it seemed real, until I
saw those eyes.

Did Matthew Shepard feel the same?

He got into their car, he couldn't have known they wanted to hurt
him. When did that change? Was it fast, all of a sudden, or did it start
in his gut and creep through his skin? Did he try to get out? What did
he think when they pulled out a gun? Did he beg them? Will he remember being tied to the fence, seeing them climb back in the car and
drive away?

Did he think they'd come back? Was he conscious? Did he see their
eyes?

Will he remember? I didn't, not until now.

When did he know he was alone?

He cried, that much is clear — the tears made tracks down his face.
What did he think in those dark morning hours? Did he see the glow of

day on the mountains? Feel the cold? What were his thoughts before sunrise?

Before the alley, I didn't understand that people could stop being human and still live. That a mother could decide not to love her child. That a stranger could want to kill you for being who you are. That there are people who breathe and walk and speak and live and do not care about other people at all. People who cannot see.

Like tricks who go with little boys.

Like the skinheads.

Like the men who passed me and turned their heads.

Like my uncle.

Like my mother.

When I understood this, all those years ago, my heart broke, and because the pain was more than I could take, I stopped crying. I wrapped up the tears and hid them away where I could forget it had even happened.

Matthew Shepard dies and my heart breaks again.

This time, I won't stop my tears. I can't.

I'll cry for the young murdered boy, for his family, for his last moments, for the truth he was forced to see before he died, for the fact that the two men live, and he does not.

I'll cry for myself. For all the children whose mothers cannot love them. For boys who are gay and must hide. For hearts so hard they can't feel their own pain, much less anyone else's. I'll cry because we are here such a very short time, and while we are here, we can choose.

Because of Matthew Shepard, I am changed.

I touch my forehead often now. I comb my hair to the other side, so the scar will clearly show. I won't hide it anymore. I won't hide me, not even when I'm afraid, not even when it seems easier to hate.

I won't choose hate. I can't.

Because I know what happens. I've seen eyes as they disconnect.

Because Matthew Shepard died, and I did not.

If my heart must break each and every day, brand-new, for the rest of my life, so be it. I will not hate another human being. I will never again forget.

# May, 2005

## LOS ANGELES

Close up, the guy's huge. He eases himself into the plastic chair, sets his coffee down, and rubs a big hand over his shaved head. He puts his cane between the plate glass and the table, but doesn't loosen his grip on it. My skin turns cold. What the hell was I thinking? I don't like skinheads, even outside Coffee Bean in broad daylight, with all these people around us.

"Hi," I say.

He nods and glances at me briefly, and dumps sugar into his cup.

I tell myself to relax. He's an *ex*-skinhead. He got all those tattoos ages ago. Isn't he at the Museum of Tolerance, just like me? Isn't he here to help me out? Whatever — my hands are sweating. I perch on the edge of the chair and keep a clear line to the street.

"Avra wants me to bring a group to your lecture next Friday," I say, managing a smile. "If that's okay with you?"

"Yeah, sure, Friday's good." He glances over again, then taps his cane lightly on the concrete. Sweat trickles down my sides.

"So, what do you talk about, specifically?"

"Oh, you know, my old lifestyle, why I left it, how I left it, and —" He cuts himself off and shrugs. His face clouds, like I'm making him mad. Or maybe he doesn't like gay men.

"Okay, and?"

"Okay, and, I don't know — I try to get kids to see how your choices can screw you up. I tell them all the stupid things I did and —"

For a brief second, I hold his stare.

His eyes are very blue.

He turns away slightly and continues.

"You mighta heard — I did some pretty violent shit. At clubs, out on the street. And there was this place we'd go a lot, down on Santa Monica and —"

"Martel," I interrupt. "Oki Dogs." The cup in my hand is shaking, I set it down.

This is not possible.

"Yeah," he replies. He taps the cane again, harder.

"Skinheads hung out there a lot." I can't feel my legs. I need to throw up.

"Yeah, pretty much always after we went clubbing."

"So you were only there on weekends?"

"No. Thursdays too."

*The biggest demon of all stands with laser eyes boring down. "He's not out yet?!"*

"We beat a kid up there once. Real bad."

"A gay kid." I grip the edge of my chair. I will not run.

"Yeah." He draws his cane toward him, looks away. A vein pulses on his temple.

I press my lips together. I drop my head. The cane raps harder, again and then again.

I lift my head and meet his eyes. I ask:

"Do you know who I am?"

"Yes."

I knew him the second I sat down. The eyes. I couldn't look at them. Now I can't look away. He stands, grabs his jacket, and stomps off. Just stomps off. The buzzing in my head kicks to a roar; rubbing doesn't help. Every possible outcome presents itself and none of them are good. I sit still a minute to gather myself. I get out a pain pill and take it with my coffee. My hand's shaking.

Why does this shit happen to me?

I don't know how I make it home. How I call the twins' mom and tell her to keep them for the night. I do know that what I'm feeling is dangerously close to out of control, that I'm going to have to work carefully to get through this one. I'm feeling like I did in jail, like I did way back in the day, when what I needed more than anything was to kick somebody's face in.

I could kick somebody's face in RIGHT NOW.

This is impossible. This can't be real. When do I get a break? How much fucking harder am I supposed to work to make something come out right?

I know I'm getting fired. I know that.

I know there's nobody in my world now who'll understand that shit like this happened all the time. He just shoulda stayed at the burger place. Why the hell did he cross that street?

I didn't know what I was doing. I was too wasted. I never saw him as a little kid—he wasn't a kid to me, he was the invader—and I honestly didn't mean to hurt him that bad, just get him out of our—

Suddenly the roar in my brain stops.

He was the same age as my son is now . . .

Everything inside me caves in, collapses. I don't know what to do.

### FRIDAY

"I made stupid choices because I didn't realize that everything I did was going to have an effect on someone. *Including* myself. You can't do violence without paying a price."

I'm midway through my presentation. The kids are watching hard to see if I'm telling the truth. This is *his* group, but he didn't show. I'm winging it on my own.

The door at the back of the auditorium opens and *he* slips through. My heart takes off. I look straight at him. He freezes, but holds my stare. My mouth goes dry.

"You know, I hurt a lot of people." My throat closes, I'm barely getting the words out. "And one of them just walked through that door." Suddenly the place is silent. The kids turn, stare. He doesn't move, but his eyes—it's like that night. Suddenly, there's no one here but him and me. I still don't know what to do.

My voice is now barely more than a whisper. But it fills the entire room.

"Dude. I'm sorry."

# AFTERWORD

## FROM HATE 2 HOPE

Matthew Boger (Jason) is often asked if he's truly forgiven Tim Zaal (Doug).

"I have. But it took a long time. I had to discover what it means to forgive someone who's done such a terrible thing. But really, it's not about helping the *other* person; it's about healing yourself. Until you forgive, that person holds power over your life. I needed to own my *self*, so I forgave. Not only Tim, but my mother too."

Tim is asked if people can really change.

"Yes, they do, I'm living proof. But it's a conscious thing. If you don't see the problem, you walk around in a delusion. Until you admit what you've is done wrong, you can't change it. I have to separate myself from the person I was in that alley, because even now, when I'm angry or feel stereotyped, victimized — I can slip into that kick-your-ass skinhead attitude. I have to keep that guy in check. I know that. I have to look objectively at the situation so I can talk about it."

"When we first started FROM HATE 2 HOPE," Matthew says, "I was afraid when I told a roomful of people I'm gay, they'd get up and leave.

But there's nothing wrong with me. I'm not broken, I don't need to be fixed. People who hate are broken. So as hard as it is to tell our stories, we do it."

I ask Matthew and Tim what they'd like people to take from our book.

Matthew says: "I'd like them to walk away with a true, deep understanding of the word *respect*. To realize that it's okay to respect others even if you disagree with their beliefs or their lifestyles. My being gay is a very small part of who I am. When you respect people you open the door to seeing who they really are. That's a stepping-stone to acceptance."

Tim agrees: "It's the essence of being American. Without respect, you have nothing. You can't have dialogue without respect, and more than anything now, we need a dialogue. All the things that happen in the schools — riots, guns, kids killing kids, killing themselves — might not have happened if people could see each other. When you respect others, you don't bully, you see. It's hard to hate what you understand. People have to start somewhere to go to the next point. We hope this book will be a beginning. An introduction."

# AUTHOR'S NOTE

September, 2006—I was back teaching theater and casting my first show when my agent called. Had I read the article in the *LA Times* about the ex-skinhead and the gay man? I had. Would I be interested in weaving some of their experiences into a story?

Are you kidding?

We met at the Paradigm Agency—I was interviewed by Lucy Stille, Avra Shapiro, and the two men—Tim Zaal sat to my left, silent, watchful, and intimidating; Matthew Boger smiled from across the table, his eyes never leaving my face. (He told me a year later he needed to see if he could trust me. He did.) We got to work.

Matthew began by outlining the events he most clearly remembered. Tim told me how the Punk movement had given him a place to fit in. I listened to Tim's playlist of Punk Rock, watched every film I could find, and visited his old stomping grounds, trying to see it through his sixteen-year-old eyes. I flew to San Francisco and walked down Polk Street late at night, hung out in The Castro, sat in Union Square—all the while imagining thirteen-year-old Matthew.

I wrote from four until six thirty each weekday morning, before going to teach, then nonstop on weekends. I started the story thirteen different ways. None of them worked. Tim and Matthew were telling as much as they remembered, but children who are compromised must hide the most dangerous things from themselves in order to survive.

One Sunday afternoon, I suggested an acting exercise. Tim and Matthew retold the incident in the alley in *present* tense, relating only what they experienced through their five senses. For example, "We get out of the car and the air's cold on my face. I hear a motorcycle go by. There's a bitter taste in my mouth and throat, etc." The intent was to bring immediacy to the experience. It worked.

Later that week, I met Matthew on the corner of Santa Monica and Martel, where Oki Dogs used to be. He pointed out where he'd first seen the skinheads march across the street. He walked me through the parking lot to where they'd caught him. I crouched down as he had, curled in a little ball on my knees, holding my head. I sat against the concrete barrier and imagined waking up there, beaten and alone. The night rushed in. I went home and wrote it. Jason and Doug were born.

The core of Jason's story tumbled out in early summer, in three weeks of nonstop writing in a house in Cambria, where an eager muse woke me each morning at six to pour words through my fingers into my laptop. I sat by the ocean and wrote until my eyes hurt. They were ten-hour days, but glorious.

Doug refused to show up. I wrote 150 pages about him, and my agent wisely sent it back (key word: about). I needed to find the little boy so I could find the teen who had so much hate. Tim and I got back to work. He shared his fears and hopes, the wish that some adult had taken the time to see him. Doug peeked out. My husband's insightful comments helped me connect the dots. I took advice from my agent Bonnie, her assistant Sarah, my editor Alvina, and my dear friends Anne and Shelly. Doug finally showed up.

I reordered chapters and cut pages and pages of story. I created characters and situations, stringing together bits of Tim's and Matthew's experiences, shaping them with details from my imagination, until finally, *Freaks and Revelations* emerged. The incident in the alley is absolute fact. All else is a work of fiction. Even so—Matthew and Tim thanked me for telling a story that they feel captures the heart of their experiences.

But it's me who has received the greatest gift—the friendship of these two remarkable men, and the chance to witness the effect that they have in the world. Matthew Boger and Tim Zaal intimately understand the devastation hate causes. They know the healing power of forgiveness and love. They believe that there is always a choice.

I believe it now too.

— D.W.H.

# ACKNOWLEDGMENTS

I am indebted to the following people:

To my (now) good friends Tim Zaal and Matthew Boger—who trusted me to tell their stories, and taught me much more than they know.

To Bonnie Nadell of Fred Hill Bonnie Nadell Literary Agency—for her wisdom, dedication, and guidance (and for suggesting me in the first place!).

To the lovely Lucy Stille of Paradigm Agency, who got it all going.

To Little, Brown Books for Young Readers and their gifted team: Alvina Ling, Connie Hsu, T. S. Ferguson, Melanie Sanders, Ben Mautner, Carolina Alvarez, and Eric Rayman.

To Avra Shapiro and Marcial Lavina at The Museum of Tolerance, for ongoing support.

To Bob Riddle and Liz Resnick at Crossroads School.

To Sarah Lagrotteria, for her many insightful contributions.

To Marcia Meier of the Santa Barbara Writers Conference.

To my first readers (and dear friends) Virginia Russell, Margie Belrose, and David Listenberger.

To Anne and Shelly Lowenkopf, for their belief in this project (and me), and to Anne for her astute, spot-on editing.

To Carol Evan McKeand, always.

To Colleen and Lew Ross, just because.

And forever to my beautiful daughter and best friend, Frazier—and her dad, my husband and soulmate, Gene Marc Hurwin.